THE RIVERS LEAD HOME

AND OTHER STORIES

EMILY HAYSE

The Rivers Lead Home and Other Stories by Emily Hayse

emilyhayse.com

Cover design by James T. Egan www.bookflydesign.com

ISBN: 978-1-733-24282-0

CONTENTS

In memory of Estella Mae Hayse, who was proud of me for becoming an author

and to Willow.

AN ABUNDANCE OF COURAGE

1

AN ABUNDANCE OF COURAGE

Blood. That was the smell filling the spring air that should have smelled of growing grass and pine.

I knew the smell of blood. Better, probably, than these men who made others bleed with their bullets and gunpowder. It was a necessary part of life. But as I lay in the grass, my shoulder burning from a bullet crease, the end of my broken spear still clutched in my hand, all I could think was that we didn't need more blood.

Our land had enough of our blood without these invaders spilling it for us.

Smoke whisked over the ground littered with broken bows, broken tents, broken men. In the morning we had fought, and in the afternoon we had suffered and died. We had taken some of their lives, but in return, they had taken nearly all of ours.

My mother had told me that this would be so. "Kavik," she had said, "the pack will not come back. You, promise me, come back." I had told her that her fears were unfounded, but she had been right.

And now I was alone, lying in the empty stillness before dusk. Alone in a field of desolation.

If I didn't move soon, I knew I'd lose my chance.

I sat up, head swimming. I must have been struck in the skull, but I have no memory of it. I couldn't look closely at the bodies lying still and stiff—once my countrymen, now nothing. At least, nothing that will feel anymore. Just memories.

My knife was lying in the grass by my feet. I picked it up, dirty as it was, and shoved it into my belt. I stood and looked around me, my body protesting at the effort.

A thin silver line to the south marked the sea, the sea over which the invaders came in their mighty boats. It had started out friendly enough. Too many questions, I hear. About the land and furs, about gold and silver, and then—like the silent hostility that passes between dogs and turns a cautious sniff to flashing teeth and snarls—it had turned ugly.

I don't know what it was, or why friendship turned to hostility. By the time the call had come to Tansilet, it hadn't mattered. Our land needed defending, and defend it we would.

So we went. And died. All except for me, it seemed.

One of the invaders' beasts wandered the edge of the field, its leather harness askew, the strips of leather to lead it trailing on the ground.

I started for it slowly. If I could stalk a *pannik* to kill, I could catch a tamed beast.

It picked its head up and regarded me cautiously, but didn't retreat. I took another step forward, trying not to look at the bodies littering the ground around me.

The ground shifted beneath me suddenly. A low cry sounded and I nearly fell over the long, wounded frame of a man.

The horse jerked its head and started away.

I shouldn't have looked down. I shouldn't have looked at his face, but I did.

He was one of the Invaders. Young—younger than I, with hair the color of deerhide and a lean, twisted face.

I couldn't help it. At the sight of his face, I growled and reached for my knife.

He scrambled back, but one leg was dragging. He couldn't go more than an arm's length. So he waited, braced, ready for me to kill him.

He wasn't going to ask me to spare him, and that is what stayed my hand.

I could have done the thing easily with my knife. A few hours before, at each other's throats, I could have done it without thinking. To me, killing him would be nothing. But to him, his life was everything.

I bent down, wiped the bloody blade off in the grass, and sheathed it.

"I wouldn't dirty my knife with you." I straightened and spat into the soiled grass.

He looked away.

Dark was falling quickly. Spring is that way—making you believe it is summer and then plunging you into a winter darkness in a matter of minutes.

"I am not asking for your help," the man said through shut teeth. "But why didn't you kill me?"

"Perhaps I should do it now," I replied, hate flaring up inside me at the sound of his voice. But it was an empty threat. To kill him would be like shooting more of a roving herd than you could take. Shooting for the pleasure, not for the need.

It would be wrong.

He sensed my reluctance to carry out the threat, and new respect entered his eyes. But any relief he felt was groundless. I would leave him, and with that hurt leg, the wolves would find him before the night was out.

Killing him would be more merciful, but at least this way, his blood wasn't on my hands.

I stepped over him and made for the horse, who lingered a few yards away.

It was not easy getting close to it or throwing my long leg over its back, but I managed. I gave it a kick, and it sprang forward.

Then the first howl came, long and lonely, and filled the fading night.

The horse shivered under me and blew through its nose like a *tuttik*.

And then, at the very worst time to remember, I remembered. The first time the cry of a wolf made me afraid, I was ten and hunting at night. I remembered how the chills ran up my arm and I looked to Sila, five winters older (and now lying dead back on that field), feeling the kinship of another shoulder beside mine to stand against this savage land.

And I could not get the hated, pain-twisted face of that Invader boy out of my head.

I turned the horse back toward the field.

It was the last and only time I would grant quarter.

He had begun to crawl across the field, but he had

made less than a man's length in the time I was gone, and I knew what wolves did to *tuttik* calves and wounded deer who moved swifter than that.

I was as much his enemy as he was mine, but there was an inevitable kinship in being the only two yet alive in this hostile land.

As much as I hated him, I knew what my choice had to be.

The wolf howled again, lonely and savage, and its kin answered from all directions. The horse snorted and stepped sideways.

I slid off its back, hanging tight to the long strips of hide that controlled it. It reared back, swinging round like a tethered boat trying to whisk downstream.

"The wolves, they'll do you in within the hour," I said, when I had convinced the beast to settle down.

"Wolves?" The man made a gesture toward the trees.

I nodded and held out my free hand. "You will share my fire tonight."

Hope lit his face, and I liked it even less that way.

"I can't stand," he said, regretfully.

I seized his arm, dragged him up, and shoved him with some effort onto the horse. He sagged against its neck.

I walked the beast upwind about a mile. Once far enough away from the carnage that we would not be in danger from smelling like it, I tied the horse to a tree and built a fire by the light of the *kitya-nitkas.* Not until it was large enough to hold off a pack did I pull the man off the beast and bring him to the fire.

"I think it's broken," he volunteered. "My ankle."

With the prospect of a night of fending off wolves

ahead, his ankle was the least of my worries. I would keep him alive for one night. After that his life or death would be on his own head.

More from curiosity than any desire to help, I cut off his boot for him. The ankle was too swollen for anything else.

I had a small pouch of provisions, just dried meat, and I tossed a piece to him.

We ate in silence.

The wolves howled on, but I knew their song. They were not hungry. After another hour of silence between us, I was sure that we would not be seeing them tonight.

I checked once more that the horse was secure, then drew my knife, putting it in the soft dirt by my head. The man could do me no harm in his condition. The day had done its work on him. He was already lying down beside the fire, and if he tried anything, I would hear.

He drew himself up on his elbow and I sat up again, my hand stealing to the knife out of habit.

"*Kuy—Kuyanak,*" he said in a low voice, with all the wrong tones.

I gave a grunt of scorn and shook my head. His thanks was empty, and my comrades were dead.

He was asleep when I woke, with the dawn. The horse was there, the fire just coals. A mist hung about the tall grasses, coming from the hills just beyond us.

I picked up my knife, sheathed it, and stood regarding the soldier for a long moment. It was likely that in the years to come, I would regret this. With every new outrage and oppression, I would remember this and wish I had not done it.

But it was done.

His face was lined and drawn, but I knew the face of a survivor. If he was one of our own, he'd be a fighter, and that we had in common.

I undid my pouch, my hands rebelling against my heart, and dropped it on the ground beside him. It might be a while before anyone found him.

I went to the horse to untie it.

"Stop right there."

A hard click of two, three pistols. A man with grayed hair stepped out of the trees, two others at his side.

For a single moment I thought of my knife. Then I thought better. I stepped away from the horse.

"What do you think you're doing with that horse?"

I stood my ground, said nothing, hardly moved.

They noticed the soldier laid out beside the fire. "What did you do to him?"

I gave a short, derisive laugh. Didn't feed him to the wolves, nothing more.

The injured man opened his eyes and dragged himself up on one arm, touching his forehead with the other.

"Sergeant Norman, forgive me for not standing. Let him be." He nodded to me.

"Who is he?"

"I don't know. But he saved my life. Let him have the horse."

The sergeant shifted his feet like a dog preparing to stand its ground, but his voice dropped, low and rough. "Thought you were dead."

"I would have been. Those wolves—" He shuddered. If

he hadn't understood the danger the day before, he did now.

The sergeant looked at me. "You did it for an enemy?" He knew as well as I how the battle had gone.

"Yes. And he is still my enemy. But the wolves do not care."

Something crossed the man's face that I did not understand, like a ripple going over a lake.

"All your people are the same. You have an abundance of courage—you lack only the power of our weapons. But that may carry you through yet. You are the kind that I wish I could fight alongside, not against."

"I have no such wish," I said. "We did not start this fight."

He nodded. "And I am sorry for that."

I spat hard and looked him straight in the eye. How could he be sorry?

But for what it was worth, he thought he was sorry. The young soldier held out his hand to me—in thanks, I think—but I only looked hard at it, and then at him.

He withdrew it, toying instead with the buttons on his shirt. Fool.

"Take the horse," he urged.

So I did.

I untied the horse from the sapling. There was no sound from the handful of men, but I felt their eyes still watching me.

I walked through them like a bear through a stream, and they parted to let me pass. There was no friendship between us, but a touch, for the moment, of respect.

I turned my back on them and set my face to the steep hills where Tansilet was nestled. I would think no more on that soldier, of how I saved from the land's due vengeance one of those who killed my brethren.

It was a secret I would carry to my grave. From now on, it was war for me and nothing but war.

When I reached the hills, I let the horse go.

THE HERO OF CHÀLKANUPA

2

THE HERO OF CHÀLKANUPA

"Ah, this bloody heat!"

Fredrick Rush leaned against the scratchy bark of the *gari* tree and fiddled with the collar of his shirt as if he wanted to rip it off.

Jeremiah calmly waved away a buzzing insect (his only annoyance was that it kept coming between his face and the tiny hills he was making) and dipped his pen into a shallow trough of ink. After one of the men had knocked over his inkstand and lost half of his precious ink in a matter of seconds, he had learned to pour out a little and work from the small amount. He could not afford to endanger his meager supply.

"The sun goes down, and yet the heat does not let up. If it were not so damp!"

"I'd jump in that river if it weren't for the flesh-eating fish," muttered one of the men, Wade.

Jeremiah laughed under his breath and reached out to dip his pen again.

"What, do you think that's funny, boy?" In a few slow

strides, Wade stood over the young mapmaker, his foot an inch from the ink.

"No." Jeremiah glanced up and removed his ink from the deliberate danger.

Rush pushed back his curly hair and came over. "Then what were you laughing about?"

Jeremiah shrugged. "I don't know."

"I don't know, *sir*," put in Wade, jerking his head in Rush's direction. "Least you can do, him being royalty."

"Sir," Jeremiah amended, giving Rush an honest nod. His refusal to join the sour mood, however unconscious, broke the tension.

Rush broke into a wide grin that betrayed his own relative youth. "Not really royalty."

"Just the king's grand-nephew."

"On the queen's side," added Rush. "In any case, I prefer the title gentleman adventurer."

"All right, men!" Sergeant Nolan came shoving his way through the brush. "Get moving on making camp. Captain'll be back soon."

He paused, looking over Jeremiah's shoulder.

"That's the river?"

"And the hills to the west bank." Jeremiah glanced up with a brief smile. "I am obliged to you, convincing the captain to let me scout it out."

"Not at all." Nolan's pale blue eyes crinkled at the corners and he slapped the boy on the shoulder. "You're a good lad."

Jeremiah gave a rare grin and returned to his work as the camp took shape around him. A fire from green wood spread smoke over the thin riverbank, and the smell of cooking meat accompanied it shortly thereafter.

"Well, Nolan, it's your lucky day."

Innes materialized through the trees. The heat had managed to get to him as well—his coat was gone, and half the buttons were open on his sweat-stained linen shirt. "I want you to head out early. By my judgment, we won't reach the rapids until late tomorrow. We can make camp and portage the following day. Hear that, Lawson?"

Jeremiah looked up and nodded.

"You'll go with Rush and Nolan tomorrow. That way you can mark your observations while we travel."

"I can help," offered Jeremiah. "I'll remember them in my head."

"No need. I want the best mapping of this territory. There's no telling when anyone will come back here. Understood?"

Jeremiah saluted. "Of course, sir. Whatever you say."

THE BROWN, wide water swept along beneath the low-bottomed hull of the dugout, murky and menacing. Jeremiah watched the way the paddles made eddies and whirlpools, harmless imitations of the deadly river itself.

The growth on the edge of the river was thick, with vines and trees trailing into the dark water. Strange animal cries followed them all day, but nothing like the noises they heard at night.

Monkeys, mostly, Nolan had said of the daytime noises. No one dared speculate about the night ones.

But it was the river that was the most frightening. The murky water hid small, flesh-eating dragons that seized upon anything that dared wander into the river and ate it to the bone, and fish the size of canoes that would swallow a man whole. Besides that, the whirlpools and rapids could catch a boat and capsize it, sucking a man under never to be seen again.

Most of the men breathed a sigh of relief whenever evening camp was reached, happy to share space with the night noises if it kept them away from the murky depths.

But neither the river nor the jungle bothered Jeremiah much. The river and the land around it were challenge enough in paper form, and that was what he was here for.

The roar started so softly that he couldn't say when exactly it had started. By the time he noticed, it was growing.

"Mr. Nolan, that sounds like rapids," he said, capping his ink. If it was, he certainly didn't want the ink open.

"You're right. We must be further downriver than we thought. Mr. Rush, turn the boat."

"Very good, sir." Rush glanced over his shoulder, switched his paddle to the other side. The boat began to pick up speed, as if drawn by a magnet to the rapids.

"Easy does it, keep it turning," urged Nolan. "Head for the bank at an angle—don't fight it."

Beneath them, the boat gave a strange twist, as if fighting back.

"Mister Rush, turn the boat." Nolan's voice was tight.

"I am trying!" Rush paddled harder, but his efforts seemed to do nothing.

Jeremiah began to pack up his tools, stuffing them back in his bag.

"Mister Rush, this is a matter of—"

The boat jerked downward and hit a rock below the water. Jeremiah lurched forward.

"Shove!" shouted Nolan.

The boat flipped.

Brown water rose to meet Jeremiah's face. He managed to get the strap of the pack over his neck before the river closed over him, twisting and turning. Muffled shouts from above echoed in his ears.

He broke the surface, gripped the rocking boat. Nolan was scrambling up the rocks on the far side of the bank. The river had spit him out far beyond them. Rush, clinging to the other side of the boat, was white as a sheet. "Jeremiah, help—"

The boat was caught in the rapids, lashing and bobbing like a spooked horse, dragging them in its wild course.

"Help!" Rush shouted, his voice cutting in and out with the wild river.

The rocks tumbled them head over heels, and Jeremiah had only one thought—hold onto the boat.

The roar of the rapids closed in.

Jeremiah dragged himself out of the murky water, clutching his bag in on hand and the tether for the boat in the other. His head swam and burned—he leaned his face into the nearest steamy cluster of bushes and was sick with all the river water.

He straightened, wiping his mouth, and glanced back. Rush was following.

"You all right, sir?" Jeremiah looked at the man limping out of the shallows, the water running from his clothes in heavy streams.

"A moment." He collapsed on the sand and began to retch.

"Lucky for both of us." Jeremiah pulled the boat in hand over hand until it was halfway up on the bank.

Rush threw himself down on his back, panting, his chin pointed to the green canopy above. "I hope I never have to live through that again."

"It's a good thing you lived through it the first time." Jeremiah opened his bag and started to pull out his sodden materials.

"How far down do you suppose we are?"

Jeremiah shook his head. "Couldn't say. We sure hit those rapids the captain was talking about. They weren't as far off as he thought."

"Blast. What luck."

Jeremiah continued to lay out his papers and tools to dry.

"What are you doing?"

"Drying my things. We'll have to wait for the others anyway—I can ink our progress in if I can get this dry."

"Wait?"

"I don't see much point in trying to go against the river. It will take them time to come around the rapids on foot, but they'll pass us eventually, I expect, and we can join back in. Besides, you look like you need the rest."

Rush grinned miserably. "I feel like I swallowed half the river."

Jeremiah regarded his things with a slight scowl. "Perhaps I should start a fire."

"I will help." Rush rolled over and dragged himself up. "Do you have flint?"

Jeremiah dug in his bag and produced it.

"Throw it here." Rush caught it out of the air. "I'll go get some firewood."

. . .

Two days had passed—lean days, as they had lost the provisions from the boat. Jeremiah had found some edible fruit a little bit inland, and Rush had netted a fish, but it wasn't much, especially after being sick from swallowing so much river water.

"They should have been here by now." Rush threw a stick into the river. A shadow moved slowly below it, betraying the presence of some hungry creature. The river whisked the twig away and the shadow disappeared.

Jeremiah corked his inkwell and began to dry his pen with a fistful of sand. "I think we should go on."

"Go on? Alone?" Rush gave a sharp laugh.

Jeremiah put the pen away and wrapped his arms around his knees.

"I mean it. I came here to map, and I can still do it. Maybe even find the sea."

"Just us?" Rush shook his head. "How will we survive?"

Jeremiah let out his breath softly, staring at the glum water. "How else will we? If they were coming, they'd have been here by now."

"Maybe they ran into trouble? They had to make the portage. Perhaps something broke."

"We weren't many miles ahead of them. They must have taken a fork further up."

"You mean—"

Jeremiah continued to stare at the flowing river. "They probably think we're dead."

. . .

For ten days, they dared the river by day and camped ashore at night, never sighting the others. They thinned under their loose shirts, both lean to begin with and finding little in the way of food.

Tonight, the boat was pulled up under a tangle of vines. Rush had taken the gun and gone into the jungle, and Jeremiah stood beneath a towering tree, peering upward, his face darkened in a thoughtful scowl. The greenery above was thick, blocking out all but a thin trickle of evening sun, yet promising far off open skies.

It was the open skies Jeremiah was contemplating.

A gunshot went off, near enough to be heard, too far to be a danger, but he neither moved nor shifted his gaze. It wasn't until Rush came crashing through the underbrush at his elbow that Jeremiah pulled his gaze from the trees above.

"If I was a jaguar, you'd be dead. You stood like a stone while I came upon you."

"I knew it was you," said Jeremiah absently, taking one last glance upwards. "What's that?"

"It's a peccary. It'll make good eating." Rush gestured with his knife to the prickle-haired brown body.

"Hm."

"Well, aren't you going to thank me? These are hard to kill."

"You used your gun."

It wasn't really an argument, simply an observation. Jeremiah tended to make them, and most men did not know what to make of them when he did.

"Well, yes, but the men say they are dangerous when provoked. And this one was certainly provoked." Rush tossed his hair out of his eyes. "Now, how about you? Is the boat secure?"

"Yes."

"Do you want to help me build a fire? We'll eat sooner."

Jeremiah tilted his head back to the green canopy overhead. "I was thinking of climbing that tree."

"Climbing it?" Rush gestured to the impossible height. "It'll take you hours, and then you'll die for your efforts. No thanks. You are staying on the ground."

"We have daylight left. It might be important. See how the land lies, maybe even spot a fire from the others."

That caught Rush's attention. "You think you could?"

"Only one way to find out."

"Wait, I'll get a rope from the boat. At least you can give yourself a little help."

While Rush went for the rope, Jeremiah dug around in his bag, stuffing a notebook in his belt and his ink bottle into his pocket.

Rush returned, a coil in his hand. "How do you want it?"

Without a word, Jeremiah took the rope, tying one end around his waist and looping the rest over one arm. Then he thrust his pen into his teeth and began to ascend.

"You're taking a notebook and pen? What if you spill the ink?" Rush laughed. But of course, with a pen in his teeth, there was no answer from Jeremiah.

"I'll just clean the peccary, have the fire started," Rush shouted up after him. "Mind you don't break your neck!"

THE FIRE CRACKLED, a comforting sound. But the peccary, its juices hot and spitting into the fire, smelled better than anything.

"Are you going to eat?" Rush looked up from the haunch he was cutting from the animal.

"Yes, in a minute." Jeremiah spoke around the pen in his mouth.

"Aren't you starved?" Rush popped a piece into his mouth.

"Yes, but I really should finish sketching this before I lose the light. There was a lot to see up there."

Rush leaned his arms over his updrawn knees. "I've never seen anyone who works like you."

"Really?" Jeremiah looked up, momentarily curious.

"You work like someone's got a gun to you."

Jeremiah smiled, amused. "Hardly, sir."

"No, I mean it. How old are you?"

"Sixteen next spring." Jeremiah stuck his pen in his mouth and flipped through his book.

"A bit young to be out here, in the wilds, doing all the mapping?"

Jeremiah shrugged. "I started when I was fourteen. Mapped the whole Nuvian frontier."

"At fourteen?"

Jeremiah looked up. "Yes."

"Not an apprentice?"

"I was apprenticed at five. Did nine years of it."

"Ah."

"I have a hope that the sea may not be far off. I couldn't tell exactly, but the eastern horizon looked a little different."

"You might have seen the sea, and you're only just telling me?"

Jeremiah glanced up but made no answer.

Rush broke a piece of meat off and held it out. "No

arguments. Eat. You'll faint before you're done inking it all in."

Jeremiah hesitated.

"Oh, come on. Someone has to make you eat. I'll make it an order if I must."

Slowly Jeremiah smiled and took the meat.

They ate in silence for some time, with just the crackling of the fire and the rush of the river for company.

"What is it that you want out of life, really?" Rush indicated to the papers with a careless hand. "Are those papers so important to you?"

"The maps? I suppose so. It's the work that's important."

"Why?"

Jeremiah bit his lip and scowled to think. "I suppose because I love it," he said after a long moment.

"You suppose?"

"I love it," Jeremiah said with more conviction, as if Rush were reaching out to snatch his work from him.

"Just the work, not fame or money? Why, you could be famous, mapping all this, if you tried."

Jeremiah just shrugged.

Rush laughed. "You are an odd one, but I have to respect that."

Jeremiah took a slow bite. "And you?"

"I don't know. I wander because I am restless. Because I can."

Again, Jeremiah shrugged.

"You know I—almost envy you. Happy where you are. In the middle of nowhere, half starved, and happy because you can keep mapping. Do you know a man might own the world and still not find what you have?"

Jeremiah was licking his fingers, picking his pen back up. Rush did not ask for an answer.

THE NEXT MORNING, Jeremiah woke to find Rush not on his watch, but facedown in the sand beside the dying ashes.

"Rush. Rush!"

The man breathed, but he was flushed and hot. Fever.

It was bound to happen to them sometime. Innes had already lost a couple men to it. But here, now, with no one else to help….

Jeremiah rolled the man over and gave him some of their precious water, bathing his face and neck in it for good measure.

Rush moaned, revived by the cooling water. "What is it?"

"You're sick. Fever."

Rush swore softly.

"Don't you worry now." Jeremiah slipped his arm under the man's neck to lift him. "You're coming with me anyway. We make it to the sea, we're out of this fever territory."

JEREMIAH'S SHOULDERS ached as if someone had seized his arms and wrenched them out of their sockets. By day he paddled, by night he pressed water on the sick man and drew his maps and charts by memory. Rush wouldn't eat, save for when Jeremiah found fruit and held tiny pieces to his lips.

He was skin and bones now, lying in the bottom of the boat, moaning and talking out of his head. The man needed rest, but not here, with the water fast and reckless and the bugs so thick they looked like clouds.

"Jeremiah?" Rush pulled himself up, looked blankly at the water moving past. "Where is this?"

"Lie down," Jeremiah said grimly, seeing nothing but fever in the man's eyes still. "We are on the river. You're sick."

"The river? Devil take the river!" Rush started up, almost capsizing the boat, knocking himself back down.

"Easy now."

"How can you say easy? How can you say that?"

"I don't understand."

"How long has it been?"

"Fifteen days."

"Fifteen days, fifteen long days of misery…." Rush trailed off, incoherent.

"We are heading towards the sea." Once they reached the sea, they could find their way up the coast to a port city.

"The sea? When will we be there?"

Jeremiah hesitated, then said very gently, "Soon."

"Soon. And I will bathe my head in the saltwater…how long have I been sick?" Rush held up a thin, bony hand.

"Maybe a week."

"Am I dying?"

"I don't know." The words felt cold in the stifling jungle air.

Rush dragged himself up again, rocking the boat. He was shaking so hard the boat moved with every tremor that ran through his body.

"I won't forget this. I won't forget this, Jeremiah. The king will hear of it. He'll make you a rich man, you'll never want for anything—"

"Just sleep, you hear? I'll get us through."

Rush laid back, his teeth set, his shoulders shaking. His eyes closed and he was quiet again.

Slowly, Jeremiah wiped his sweaty palms on his pant leg.

FAINT GRAY LIGHT flooded the river ahead of them in the dawn. Jeremiah had stopped late and started again at the first sign of light. He hadn't even left the boat—just tied it up to a thick overhanging branch. Making camp was too much effort now, and he felt, strong as a bird flying north after winter, that he had to keep going.

He was so tired now that everything was numb and pleasantly warm. There was no more pain, even though his hands were blistered and bleeding.

He had torn half of his shirt in strips the night before, bandaged his hands enough to ink in the previous day's progress. The shirt was ruined, but that didn't seem to matter.

Rush lay like a dead man in the bottom of the boat. The fever had racked his body all night, and for a long time it seemed like the end had come.

But he still breathed when daylight came, and when Jeremiah dared to reach out and touch him, his skin was cool.

"Jeremiah?" Rush didn't try to sit up. "Where are we?"

A distant roar had begun, so soft that at first Jeremiah thought his ears were playing tricks.

"Is that—is that the river roaring?" Rush whispered.

A seabird, wheeling in the misty air, called overhead, and Jeremiah didn't need to answer.

. . .

Jeremiah moved the chart he was transcribing out of the light so the ink wouldn't fade. If he took care, it might last a good while longer than he.

"What's that?" His bunkmate Lieutenant Sanborn came in and peered over his shoulder. "Still working on that old Nuvian chart?"

"The transcriber made an error, and since I have leave —" Jeremiah stuck his pen in his mouth momentarily to shift the chart— "I thought I would fix it myself."

"Leave is for resting, not doing some clod's job for him." Sanborn sat down on his cot and started to pull off his boots. "Hear about the big to-do? Lord Rush heading down to the Parmyla jungles again?"

"I did."

"Imagine, being royalty and a fearless explorer to boot. The first man to discover the Chàlkanupa passage. Do you know what the newspapers are calling him?" He paused for effect, but he was accustomed to Jeremiah and did not expect an answer. "They're calling him 'the Hero of Chàlkanupa.' Wish I had been there. Must have been something."

Jeremiah dipped his pen and wiped the excess on the ink bottle.

"I've read Rush's reports of his discovery," Sanborn persisted. "He even mentioned you, said the mapmaker saved his life in the rapids. Did you really do that?"

"Hm?" Jeremiah glanced up.

"I said, did you really save his life in the rapids?"

"Oh. I suppose." Jeremiah smiled a little and returned his attention to the papers in front of him, as if the conversation was a mere distraction. "But then, he could exaggerate at times."

BARBARIAN AND THE WAR

3

BARBARIAN AND THE WAR

The smoke catches you off guard at first.

It makes you stop and count the days backward, a thing you almost never do: back to the stay at Tompkins's cabin, back to the twelve days coming across the plain, back to the wintering home north of Tukumi.

It is too early for the fires to begin.

You listen closely, hear a rumble instead of a roar. Swallow comes up to you with a low whine, her ears pressed to her skull. You reach down and rub her ears. She has always been your best dog and has the keenest nose for approaching danger.

A sharp crack follows, like the snapping of a branch, but you are too far away from any trees for it to be a branch. It makes you think of something else—something far away and unpleasant, like the sting of smoke to your nose.

You whistle to your dogs, call them close. You sense it like a storm on the horizon. Something is wrong and it is coming for you.

The dogs perk up at the sounds and smells. You whistle low and they follow, tails wagging, noses in the grass. But you do not head southwest, toward the river where you had planned to fish and water the dogs. Instead, you angle away southeast, where in three hours you will reach the same river at another point.

The dogs can wait that long. For the time being, they are more interested in finding field mice and spring hares.

Jori raises his head and barks sharply, and Swallow jerks her head around to see. The others join, stopping and raising their heads in loud warning. But they are unsure, telling you to watch, not certain enough to attack.

Then you see them coming, riding horses, like men from a dream you used to have. Only this is now, not then, and these men wear green coats, not red.

It is almost on your lips to shout for the dogs to attack, but that would do no good. And in your heart, you do not want to do it. You don't want to think about what it reminds you of.

Instead, you call the dogs to you as you would before you enter a village, tell them to settle down. They come, happy to be called, squirming and falling over themselves in their eagerness to obey.

Like spoiled children, they have forgotten the hard work of winter hauling; they forget that sometimes they do not want to listen.

You push away the unsettled feeling that rises in your chest and you crouch down among them, telling them what good dogs they are. You cup each head that comes to you in your hands, pulling their silky ears back with your gentle stroking, kiss each head.

It is good for them to know how much you care for them.

You also want them to think that these men are not a danger, to show them that you are not afraid that they approach on their long-legged creatures.

You know what they are. You've seen animals like those long ago, but these dogs only know deer and *pannik*. Beasts often to be chased, never to be ridden.

Swallow bumps your leg, pressing against you, thrusting her nose under your arm. She is worried and telling you so.

"Easy, girl. Good girl." You press her briefly to your chest, kiss her nose. The best dogs seem always able to feel your heartbeat and know when you are calm.

Your heart is as steady as the pulsing wind pressing through the wide grasses.

One of the men cups his hand to his mouth. "Hulloo!"

This sets the dogs to barking. They are not afraid anymore, but this is a disturbance and perhaps, they think, a mockery to their own language.

Some of them, the younger and more foolish ones, probably think it a greeting of their own kind.

You laugh to yourself, speak to them a little louder than usual, and they hush.

The horses are nervous now.

It will be better for the dogs to keep their distance.

You call to them, urge them toward the southwest, but as you do so, you get a good look at the newcomers. They are lean, their green coats buttoned tight, burning in the heat of the sun.

"Hey, you! Boy!"

You stop. Not because they call you boy, though it has been a long time since anyone called you that. They are wearing guns, and you know that they wear them for a reason.

Your dogs are anxious again. They mill about you, sniffing the horses but afraid to venture too close, a few giving hesitant growls.

"You got a name?" one of the men calls out. He's got a beard, a rough voice.

You hesitate. It has been the better part of a year since you have spoken to a person. And today, you are not in the humor.

Perhaps, if you give them what they want, they will leave you alone. And that is what you want most.

If they leave, you will have peace. There is enough wild land for that.

"Barbarian."

"What?"

They can't hear you. You don't approach them, but you whistle to the dogs and the men take this as an invitation to come closer.

"What is your name?"

"They call me Barbarian."

"You a native of these parts?"

These parts is a broad statement, not really suited to the moment, but you nod.

"You don't look like them."

You shrug. "But I am."

"Born here?"

You shake your head. This stumps him.

"I don't suppose you've seen anyone?"

You smile, scratch your ear. The presence of any people makes you nervous, especially these impressive men on tall horses.

"I have seen no one but you in eight months."

He looks you up and down, finally seems to decide to believe you.

"At least you can tell me which way the river is? We're separated."

You pause. You could send them the wrong way, straight into where the brown bears, newly roused from their hibernation, are feeding—the very place you skirted with your dogs. It would serve the strangers right, disturbing you and this quiet land with their guns. You had almost forgotten about guns. You were happy to forget, and now the memories come back fresh.

Or you could point them in the right direction. They would go on their way, pursue their business, maybe pester you again sometime in the future. But they would be gone all the same right now.

"Well?" the man demands. His horse is fidgeting. Maybe it can scent, the way the *pannik* can, the bears feeding upwind from you.

"The river is to the south," you say at last, unconcerned by the man's impatience. "But ride an hour along it before you try to cross. It is swollen up here."

"You came from there?" He is skeptical, and you don't really blame him. To be foreign, seeking help from a native—they must truly be lost to ask your guidance.

"No, but it is always swollen there after the snows melt."

This is enough for him.

"Thank you." He tugs at the brim of his hat and then, as if a thought strikes him, digs in his pocket and brings out a gold coin.

"For your trouble."

You shake your head. "I don't want it." You don't want

much in life, especially not things like money that tie you down—things you must keep track of and will probably lose the next time your sled tips in deep snow.

He will make much more use of it than you will.

"Very well." He puts it back, kicks his horse. "You're the first mannerly one I've met in this big land…." His voice trails off, and you think to yourself that perhaps he hasn't been in this land long enough. You are not usually numbered among the mannerly, though you are always grateful when a trapper shares a meal or a village their fire. Surely if he went further north, he would meet some fine people….

You watch them out of sight.

Partly because you want to make sure they are headed in the right direction: away from you. Partly because you do not trust them enough to stop watching. And partly because there's a strange feeling coming over you, a going-back.

You are a very little boy again, wearing clothes made by your mother and not yourself, and you remember the taste of milk, foamy in a bowl, fresh from a cow.

A cow. You have not thought of cows in a long time. Yours had been white and brown, with eyes bigger than a deer's. You used to burrow in the hay, watching while she was milked.

You hid in the hay once—once, when the town was afraid and your father loaded his gun. That once was the only time you saw him use it.

You hear in your mind the rush of a swiftly set fire, see homesteads burning, their thatch curling like straw. You can hear, though you try not to remember them, the screams.

You remember the gray emptiness that followed.

But now the sun is warm again, the sky is blue, and

your dogs are scattered across the meadow, sniffing out the flat grass where the deer bedded and barking at the retreating figures on their horses. All but specks now, on the far end of the meadow.

You whistle to the dogs, count their swiftly moving bodies, brown, black, gray, tan, white. All the colors of the thawing ground.

And you leave those memories behind, where you left them before.

It is all right now, you tell yourself. It is over, and everything is all right.

THE RIVERS LEAD HOME

4

THE RIVERS LEAD HOME

It was the summer I was eleven, legs longer than my head and shoulders together, when Tsanu took me out many days' journey from Tansilet. It was the season for fish and berries, not for hunting, and we had been working on our fishing spears all winter.

"Maki," he had said to me, "this year I think I shall take you north towards the swifter mountain streams for our fish." He hadn't even looked at me. Just said the thing as he smoothed the shaft of his spear by the flickering firelight.

"I'd like that," I said, glancing up, unable to keep my eagerness out of my face. But I shouldn't have worried. As I said, he was looking at his spear.

We took Trout and Umuk with us to carry the extra supplies, and Tsanu and I carried our spears in packs across our shoulders. We fastened our door with the bone hooks, listening to the clamor of the young dogs who did not want to be left behind and had not yet learned the manners to be quiet, and then came the part I did not like, when we headed across the village and past the Invaders' camp.

Sometimes they came out and questioned us as to where we were going, sometimes they ignored us. They understood that in order to live, one must hunt and fish and collect roots and berries, but Tsanu was tall and strong for a young man, and he was fine-looking and well-regarded in the village, so they noticed him and stopped him more.

Today there were two young soldiers at the path that led out of the village. One was tall and pale-haired, with eyes that would have been keen if they weren't so lazy. The other was just a boy, nearer my age than Tsanu's. Too young for an army.

Trout growled in his throat as we passed, and the boy stepped back.

"Easy now, he's not going to hurt you," said the tall one with a bit of a laugh. "They're all a tad wolf, is all."

I saw a gleam in Tsanu's eyes. He knew better than to laugh, but he was laughing inside.

The tall one stepped into the path. "Where are you going?"

"Out to fish."

"Hmm." He glanced us over, from the dogs to the spears to the packs we wore. "Which way?"

"North. And east some."

The young man glanced north and east, scratching the side of his nose with a long finger. Then his gaze swung back to me. "With her?"

I gave him the haughtiest, most distrustful stare I could muster.

"She's my sister."

"Well, I don't doubt that—it's whether she's up for the journey. If that's where you're going."

I let my lip curl into a snarl and I searched a moment for a good insult. But Tsanu was too swift.

"She is strong. The journey, for her, is not hard."

The young soldier scrutinized us both another long moment and then nodded. "Very well. Good journey." He waved us on casually, almost friendly-like. I stiffened and passed as close to him as I could, so that I almost brushed him.

WE TRAVELED FOR DAYS, over hills and through meadows, giving *tuttiks* with younglings wide berths, sleeping under pines and stars and pretending we could catch the *kitya nitkas* in our hands. We woke with the sun and ate over a fire in the dusk. Like this, I was happy. These were fallow moments where sorrows and dreams didn't come and didn't belong. I could go on inside those days forever.

ONE AFTERNOON, late, we came to a place where the trees opened up to show the river far below. It wound like a shining band through a bed of dark pines, scattering banks of pebbles along its majestic way. It put me in mind of a herd of *pannik*, moving slow and strong across the land, forging its own path. Down at the river's edge stood a grove of white birch, their leaves shaking in the breeze, shimmering like the moving water.

"Did I not tell you it was worth the journey?" Tsanu turned to me and dropped his warm hand on the top of my head.

I grinned. "It was worth the journey."

"Tonight, we set up camp. In the morning, we will start early."

It took us another hour to reach the pebbly shore near the birch grove, where we set down our packs, freed Trout and Umuk from theirs, and let them run down to the water.

"Watch the dogs while I cut some wood," said Tsanu, watching them lap the water and mock-fight each other in the water.

I went down to the edge of the river and sat down on a dead, water-polished log. With wolf in their blood, those dogs would probably wander twenty miles before they even thought about coming back.

Sure enough, within ten minutes, they tired of playing and trotted at a great pace away from our campsite, their noses pressed to the earth, their tails swinging low.

I called them back, and they heeded. There was a reason we had brought them and not the young dogs.

After a while, they tired of wandering and being called back and they curled up contentedly in the shade of the birches to pant.

Tsanu came through the trees, dragging some long, sturdy branches, about as thick as his forearm. He chopped them to the right length, and I laid out the strips of hide and helped him lash them together into racks.

It was dark by the time we finished setting up camp. The dogs were tethered near the woods, the racks stood ready on the pebbly shore, and our nets and spears were laid out for the morning.

Though morning would come early, Tsanu let me sit up with him while he repaired one of the nets. I nestled up against him, my head on his shoulder, staring into the flames, feeling the comforting movement of his arms as he worked.

I must have fallen asleep, for I only have a vague memory of him laying my blanket over me and planting a kiss in my hair.

Morning started at the edge of dawn when the gray mist hovered over the river and moved over our camp like smoke. Tsanu was already awake, stacking birch and alder wood and waking up the fire. The dogs on their tethers were stretching and yawning.

"Good morning, little wolf," he greeted. "Come here."

I pushed aside my blanket and came over. The crunch of the pebbles under my feet sounded loud in the still, thick morning.

"Look what I have."

He picked up a basket with the hand that was not busy stirring the fire and I looked inside. There were berries, fresh and plump.

"Where did you find these?"

"Over the hill. They'll go fine with the *pantak*."

"Will we have time to pick more?"

"Certainly. While the fish are drying, we can take turns watching and picking. Now eat up. It's almost time."

Tsanu waded out into the rushing river, one end of the net in his hands. He had picked a place where the river narrowed between the shore and a spit of sand and pebbles partway out. The net would help trap the fish as they swam between, letting us spear them.

I watched him solemnly from the bank, my spear in my hand. I could see in my mind's eye all the fish that swam below, out of sight, and my mouth watered. We had to catch many fish to save up for winter.

"All right, Maki."

I stepped into the water, seeing the strain of Tsanu's arms as the fish pressed against the net.

"Out of your great number, I ask only what is needful," I whispered. "This is the oath I make."

I drove my spear downward, and it took all my strength to drag the struggling fish out of the water. *He's big. But I will show Tsanu how strong I am, impress him.* I dragged the fish up the bank and went back.

"Ah! Trout, Umuk!" Tsanu barked from the river, and I heard the dogs scuttle back, away from the fish. They would get their share before long.

After a time, we traded places. Tsanu was much faster with the spear than I was. He could spear a fish and throw it up the bank without shifting his feet in the river. I watched him as I braced against the net, and I was proud at how easily he caught these fish.

Because of him, we had never starved.

When we had as much fish as we could handle for the day, we pulled in the net and began to cut the fish-meat in long, thin strips, hanging it to dry.

The sun had come out. It was flashing across the moving water like the scales of fish, and a breeze was sweeping down across the wide shore. It was perfect weather for the fishing and drying.

We worked long, not talking about taking a rest, not even thinking it. You always work hard the first day, Tsanu told me. What if the fish stop? What if a bear wrecks your camp? You work the first day like it is the last day.

We were both exhausted by nightfall, with just enough strength left to cook a slab of one of the biggest fish. Tsanu and I ate our fill and there was still plenty to share with the dogs.

Full and tired, we laid down on the ground. We stared at the stars coming out and listened to the rush of the water.

Tsanu let out a long, contented sigh. "What would you think if we had our own horses?"

"What are horses?" I asked.

"The hornless beasts the Invaders have. Think how much we could carry back."

The hornless beasts.

"I wish we could," I agreed.

"They would never trade us one." Tsanu rolled over and thrust his hand under his head. I liked how his black hair ruffled like the feathers on a crow when he stuck his hand in it.

"I want to ride one."

"Do you?" His smile was white in the dim light. "If I could get you one, I would."

I had always wanted to ride something. Ever since I had seen the Invaders do it, I had imagined what it would be like. I even imagined what the wide back of a *tuttik* would feel like.

"Kavik said he rode one once," I offered.

"Did he?"

"During the war. It is how he escaped. He had never ridden one before, and he says he never did it again."

"If anyone could do it, I suppose Kavik could."

Kavik has long legs, like a *tuttik*.

"Do you think I will be tall, Tsanu?" I asked.

"I don't know. I suppose you could be. I am."

"Was Father tall?"

"Yes. But Mother was small."

There was a long, gentle silence between us.

"You should sleep, Maki," said Tsanu after a space. "We won't get much sleep while we're on the river."

He was going to get far less sleep than I would. He would be keeping an ear out for bears and scavengers all night. At least we had the dogs. They'd give us early warning if something was close.

I moved over so that my foot touched Tsanu's leg. There was something comforting about being able to feel him there as I fell asleep.

THE NEXT DAY the weather was perfect again. The sun beat down on the rocks and glinted off the moving water, and the fish were running so thick that we had more than we needed in very little time. With the strong sun and a good wind, the fish would form the dry crust needed to keep the flies off and complete the drying process.

I sliced another fish open, making swift, neat cuts around the bone and wishing I could push my hair out of my face—it was braided back, but the wind kept pulling strands loose. I glanced at the pile yet to be cut. We would be here much longer, and I was growing more and more tired of the stench. Not that I would breathe a word of complaint to Tsanu. It is hard to complain to someone who is always doing more than you, and for your sake. I sliced the meat into thin strips, pretending the oily smell was not so strong and imagining how good the oily meat would taste come winter when the snows sat halfway up our walls.

Across from me Tsanu was sweating, up to his elbows in blood and oil. I straightened, my back aching in protest, and started across the slick pebbles to hang my fish.

I was a sure-footed girl, but working with fish is slippery work. As I passed Tsanu's spot on the ground, one foot came out from under me and I landed heavily on my knee.

"Maki, you all right?"

I scrambled up quickly, my leg smeared with everything he'd been working in for the last few hours. I couldn't even tell if I had cut my knee or not.

I gave a little growl and limped down to the water to splash the dirt off the unfortunate fish. Then I limped back to the racks to hang it up, skirting Tsanu's workplace.

"Maki, is that your blood or the fish's?" asked Tsanu, looking at me with amusement.

"Probably mine," I snapped back. I was hot and displeased, mostly because I was embarrassed to have slipped. Tsanu never slipped.

"Well then." He set down his knives and stood up slowly, reaching over to rinse his hands in the edge of the river. It wasn't fair that he was so long he could just reach over to wash them.

He scooped me up even though I kicked in protest and marched straight into the river with me, depositing me on my feet, up to my waist in water.

"Tsanu!" I leaned down and splashed him with all my might.

He laughed loudly and started backward as my water hit him in the face. With one hand (being mostly a good brother), he splashed me back.

I tackled him and we both fell in the water, hitting the rocky bottom and emerging spluttering and coughing.

"Sorry." I grinned in the blinding sun as the water ran off of me. Trout and Umuk were barking, wanting to join our rough play.

He ran his hand over his face, trying to slough some of the water off. He gave a little smile. "Had enough?"

I shrugged.

"Good. I'm going to dry off."

He waded out of the water and threw himself down on the warm rocky shore, shaking out his dark hair.

I splashed after him and settled on the rocks beside him. Even in summer the water was cold. I suppose it was fed from some mountain stream.

"Where does this river come from?" I picked up a pebble and threw it into the water.

"This one is from the lower Tanaka range."

"And where does it go?"

"To the sea, eventually." He picked up a pebble, brown and greenish, and he turned it in his fingers, studying it. "But not before it runs past Tansilet."

"This does? You mean it feeds that stream out in the forest, beyond the village?"

"The very same. If we followed this river, it would take us home. But our overland route is quicker."

I let out my breath slowly. It is a thing I have to consider carefully, to fit it into my mind. The great mountains with their ice and snow feeding little streams, streams that ran into rivers that cleared great paths and moved aside rocks, rivers that fed other rivers, all leading through the heartland and out to the sea.

"I cannot believe it," I said, throwing another pebble.

"This is the same as our river, and when I put my feet into it, I am touching something that touches the Tanakas and the sea—at the same time."

Tsanu smiles, rolling the pebble in his palm.

"You see, Maki, that's the thing about the rivers. They're like the blood-lines in your hands. They carry life wherever they go, from the highest mountain snows, to the lakes in the valleys, to the white-tipped seas. They're like a map all themselves. If you lose your way, follow the river downstream and you'll always find your way back."

I rolled over to look at him. "It leads all the way to our stream? The place we always go?" He had already said it, but I wanted to hear it again.

He tossed his pebble up in the air and caught it. "All the way."

A FEW DAYS LATER, I saw the clouds. I was pulling up grass and laying it under the slippery skin of the fish so they wouldn't slip off the hanging racks we had moved up the hill for the stronger breeze, when I noticed them.

A smudge on the horizon.

I shaded my eyes and stood on my toes, gazing at the southwest.

"Tsanu, the clouds are dark."

He glanced up at me, then set his knife down.

"Where?" He trudged across the pebbly shore through the blowing smoke and up the hill to where I stood.

I pointed to where the clouds were gathering.

"It's over the mountains. We have some time."

"Enough for the fish?"

He gave a sniff, as if testing the wind for answer. "We will see."

If it rained too soon, our fish would not dry, and they would turn sour.

"What are we going to do?"

"Finish the fish for me." He started back down the hill. "There are not many. I am going to dig a dry place in the bank."

I worked as fast as I could, making quick, clean cuts and running to the racks, not walking. The sunlight would go before the rain began, and we needed that sun. The smoke would help, but without both, it would be slower.

"Maki, use the birch, not the alder wood." Tsanu glanced up at me as I passed him on my way up the bank. There was dirt on his face and in his hair, and it made me smile.

I hung the last fish and picked up an armful of the birch, putting it on the smoke-fire. Birch burned hot and small. It was better than alder with coming rain in the air.

I watched the fish carefully, keeping the smoke going, which kept off the flies and the birds. From the hill where I stood, I could see the dark clouds coming closer and closer.

A flock of geese flew over, heading away from the storm.

I watched, went down the hill to check on Tsanu and his progress, and went back to watching again. For the rest of the morning and all of the afternoon, I did this as he worked.

And the sky grew darker.

From time to time, light flashed over the distant trees and a deep rumble like a herd of *pannik* answered. Every time that happened, Tsanu stopped working and stared at the sky a few moments as if reading it.

"I will hurry," he would say. "Watch the fish."

And he kept digging.

At last he called me. There was now a large cave in the steepest side of the hill, and he was lining the inside with river rocks to strengthen it and keep it dry.

"Come give me a hand," he invited. Together we worked: I went out and brought back good flat, dry stones, and he laid them in and propped them against the sides.

At last it looked sufficient. More than sufficient, I thought. It looked like a place one would want to keep, not leave behind after a time.

"All right, we need to load all the fish."

We started with the driest meat, putting it in the back, and moved through the work of the last several days until we reached the freshest fish.

"I do not know if all of it is ready," I said, touching one of the thicker pieces.

"We cannot wait any longer." Tsanu whipped a glance up at the dark sky. "We will have to take our chances."

He climbed the bank and together we rushed the last of the dried fish down.

Rain pattered across the trees, accompanied by a wind that bent the branches, and I watched it sweep across the river, coming to us.

"Quick, Maki!" Tsanu took the last of the fish from my arms and thrust it in, then began to close up the entrance with stones. I helped him, kneeling on the stones that were quickly darkening with drops, piling them up against the windswept rain.

A few frantic minutes and the entrance was sealed.

"Maki!" Tsanu shouted over the noise of the wind. "Go to the berry bushes. Wait for me there." I ran, scrambling up the hill, ducking low as the light flashed again and the earth shook with the thundering answer.

I threw myself into the shelter of the bushes, feeling the sudden safe feeling of something over my head, imperfect as it was. The wind blew harder, bending the bushes around me, and I drew my arms around my knees, laying my head on them. It felt safer somehow.

Tsanu came running up the bank, leading the dogs by the tethers—he tied them to the base of a bush near me and they shoved their way under, thrusting their damp muzzles in my face in greeting and then hunkering down. They did not like storms.

Tsanu ducked under. "It isn't much, but it's better than the trees or the river."

I nodded and grinned. I didn't like storms much either, but with Tsanu here, it felt like nothing could go seriously wrong. It was an adventure.

He was dripping rain, as soaked as when I dunked him in the river, and his hair and shirt were plastered against him. I didn't care. I was wet too. I cuddled against him and he put his arms around me, leaning his chin on my shoulder. He smelled of fish and fresh dirt and stormy wind.

Thunder growled above us.

"Close one, little wolf?"

I nodded. I didn't need to say it—he could feel the movement. His heart was beating calmly against my shoulder blade, and I leaned back, feeling at last the warmth that comes when two bodies are close. It fought off the chill of being soaked and having a beating wind fingering its way through the bushes to your cold skin.

I thought of the fish, safe in its shelter deep under the hill, and I thought of how long it would feed us in winter-time. It was a good feeling, thinking of it.

The branches around us swayed and the rain beat in a steady drizzle through the bushes onto our necks and through our hair, but I'm not sure I have ever felt safer than I did in that moment.

TUKKULI

Tukkuli:
A word from the Koqebani meaning “a love that overcomes death.”

5

TUKKULI

It was like fate. The very day the runts were born, Spruce walked into Chegak, a total stranger. In Chegak, where there is nothing for miles around, if a man comes in to town alone and unknown, he's bound to garner some suspicion. More so when he's fair, dresses like a southerner, and carries a gun.

But such was the coming of Spruce.

He walked in wearing a thin homespun shirt under a vest, a bedroll and rifle across his back, and boots that looked as if he had walked all the way from Arislet in them. The outfitters was the only common place in town, and that's where he came upon a two-bit meal and indirectly, the runts.

Remi Attliq was in that day, collecting pay off a fine winter's haul from his line north of Kaquom, sealing the deal with a glass of imported pure.

"Who are you?" Remi turned at the opening of the door to see a strange face.

"New in town."

"That's clear." Remi cleared his throat significantly.

Tommy Two-Fingers stumped in from the back room, shaking his head. "You look cheap and poor. Get a move on before that gun of yours scares away people who actually have something to trade on them."

"Now, hold it. I haven't scared anyone with this." The newcomer lifted the strap on his bundle and ducked his head out from under it. "There. It's on the floor, if it makes that much of a difference."

Tommy grunted, dissatisfied. "Well, what do you want?"

"Is there a place to stake around here?"

"Not here," replied Tommy quickly. "No place in Chegak, not for the likes of you."

"Well, I walked weeks to get up here. They said in Ralkata that there were stakes up here. I don't need much. Just a few acres, somewhere to put a lean-to."

"Sorry." Tommy threw up a hand and stalked away, bringing the conversation to an abrupt end.

The newcomer lingered at the counter, his brow furrowed, his hands on his hips.

Slowly Remi reached down and pulled another glass from the counter, tipping half of his into it.

"Have some." Remi slid it down toward the man with his fingertips.

"Thanks." The man touched his lips to the drink and promptly coughed.

"What? This is imported. Nothing like the homemade pure out here."

"Reckon I don't drink much to start with."

Remi grinned. "Not a bad way to be. This stuff's expensive and hard to come by."

"I appreciate you sharing, then." The man gritted his teeth and finished the glass. He set it down with a clunk and reached down for his bundle.

"Now then, where are you going?"

"Look around. Is it true what he says?"

Remi pushed his black hair back from his forehead. "Tommy's suspicious. A lot of folks are when strangers show up in the middle of nowhere. This is a small town. We know everyone around these parts, and when you tote that thing—"

"There's lots of them down where I came from. Foreign and native alike."

"That's down south, or I miss my guess. Not a lot of those newfangled weapons to be found up here."

The man gave a little smile in assent.

"Truth is," —Remi lowered his voice— "there are stakes if you know where to look and who to ask."

"And?"

Remi touched his chest with a strong finger. "You've chanced upon the right man. But first—when was the last time you ate? You have too much in height and not enough everywhere else."

The newcomer shook his head and for the first time a real smile showed on his face. "I appreciate the offer, but I don't want to be beholden to you. And being tall suits me just fine."

"For outrunning trouble, maybe, on those legs, but not for lasting a winter. Come—I'll not have you think poorly of Chegak's hospitality. Tommy! A hunk of that pannik for my good friend, and a piece of bread besides."

"I'm charging," muttered Tommy, reappearing with the food.

"So be it." Remi turned to his new friend. "I can afford to be generous today. I have silver in my pocket besides all the supplies I need for the season. It's a time to be giving."

The stranger ate in silence, each movement measured and deliberate, but Remi knew the look of hunger in a man's eyes well.

"Got a name, son?"

"What's it matter?" The stranger's defenses rose slightly.

"Got to call you something."

A moment's hesitation.

"Norman."

Remi accepted this with a grunt, unbothered by the lack of a name to go before or after.

The door swung open and a short, trim, pale man tramped in.

"Halver, what can I do for you?" Tommy's attention swung away from the stranger like a bear scenting the low breeze.

"My Arrival's had her pups. Reckon you can spread the word? She's got ten, I'll probably keep five."

"Sure thing."

"How much are you selling for?" the newcomer spoke up.

Halver turned and looked him over, seeing him for the first time. "Two plew, best quality, or a silver bit. They're the best dogs."

"More than you can afford," put in Tommy pointedly.

The newcomer ignored this, rubbing his chin thoughtfully. Halver tramped out.

"News is that Atka's litter might be coming today," said Remi. "His girl's overdue by his reckoning."

"How much does Atka sell for?"

"Gold dust or whiskey. And lots of it." Tommy slammed his ledger book down on the counter. "Now be off."

Remi stepped forward as if to come between his new friend and the proprietor, but the newcomer pushed away the empty plate and turned to him, away from Tommy.

"Which way to the stakes?"

Tommy made a disapproving sound.

"Just down the street. Place with the green shutters. I'll show you the way if you give me a minute."

"No need. Thanks for the meal."

He shouldered his pack and went out.

"He's a strange one. Mark my words, he's not safe. I don't like his light hair." Tommy shook his head.

"You don't mind Halver's light hair." Remi gave a small smile and dropped a two-bit on the counter. "So long."

Tommy followed him out the door, stuffing his pipe fussily.

A handful of trappers and fisherman stood around, arms folded, watching the stranger make his way down the street, the barrel of his rifle protruding like the shaft of a broken spear.

"Who is that?" one of the trappers asked.

"Newcomer," grunted Tommy. "Won't stay long."

"You say that as he walks towards the land office." A ripple of laughter went through the men.

"Where'd he come from?"

"Didn't say." This was Remi's contribution.

"Huh." Various sounds and utterances continued the slow study of the man.

One of the trappers leaned against the wall with a grin. "That man ain't nothing but a walking spruce."

Tommy pulled his pipe out of his mouth to guffaw.

So the name stuck. No one remembered the lonely real name, or if they did, they didn't bother with it. From that day on, he was simply Spruce.

SPRUCE WAS poor as dirt except for the rifle he carried on his back, which he swapped for a spindly ten acre parcel. At first, he was determined to camp on his own land, but Remi, who had taken an odd shine to the young man, wouldn't hear of it until Spruce had something besides a lean-to of pine to sleep in. After all, he had now only a knife to his protection, and there was an abundance of bear that spring.

Remi was more than a bit surprised the day Spruce, a week or two after his arrival, walked into the cabin with two pups tucked in his shirt.

"What's this?"

"Runts." Spruce was stroking the head of one with the end of a crooked finger. "They were going to be culled. Way I figure, they might do better with someone feeding them."

"But they're too young to be weaned."

"They're weaned now," he said, glancing over. "Leastwise, I'll be their mother. Don't worry, I'll scrape up what I need."

"I wasn't thinking of that." Remi shook his dark head. "It's just that if they're being culled, I doubt you got a square deal."

"I got them for a stack of split wood each. This one—" he pulled out a wrinkled black and white pup— "is blind in one eye, see that? And this one—" he put the first pup back and pulled out a honey-colored one— "is half the size of her littermates. Wasn't going to make it much longer with them anyways."

Remi cleared his throat, unconvinced.

"And where'd you get them?"

The runts were from two different litters: the black and white pup from Halver's tan female, Arrival, and the honey-colored pup from Trapper Atka's old girl, Uumi. Little things that huffed and squeaked and could barely walk across Spruce's lap.

But true to his word, Spruce scraped up enough to feed them for the following weeks. Many a time, Remi woke to find him in front of the embers in the middle of the night, feeding them by hand. By the time they could be weaned, they were both wild little things that stumbled all over their feet and bit at Spruce's fingers when he played.

For a stranger whose knowledge of the wilderness and dogs and trapping was uncertain, Spruce raised the puppies well. Every morning he got up and held them in his hands, checking them over, talking to them.

It was not the way it was done in Uniap'nik, but Remi found it fascinating.

It was just before dawn and Remi was stirring the fire, which inevitably woke the pups. The boy, Sly Eye, stretched and yawned, then waddled off the old feed sack in the corner where they slept to the place where Spruce lay on his bedroll. The girl, Tavii, picked up her head to watch him and followed a few seconds later.

Sly Eye put his paws up on Spruce's chest and began to

lick his face vigorously, eliciting a groan. The man turned his face and Sly Eye gave pursuit.

"Now then, you little rascal!" Spruce reached up to grab Sly Eyes, causing Tavii, who had just begun to hesitantly lick his hand, to shy away.

"Easy, easy now." Spruce sat up and held out his long fingers and she came back to him, her baby tail between her legs. He scooped her up and held her to his chest, putting his chin on her fuzzy head.

"What'd you go and name her Tavii for? She's the scaredest puppy I've ever seen."

"Maybe that's why." Spruce held her up, running his hand along her back. "I want her to live up to her name—it's the scared ones that end up the bravest, you know."

"Still, you're going to get a laugh when they find out you named her courage."

Spruce set her down and snatched up Sly Eye, who was trying to bite his foster sister.

"Well, good morning, Sly." The puppy yowled in annoyance. "Hush, now, it's only a minute of your time." He held him out in front of him, regarding his stubby puppy face.

"You aren't much, are you?" The puppy tried to wriggle away, but Spruce held him fast in his strong hands. "But you will be. Mark my words, you will be." The puppy rolled its head over, trying to chew his fingers.

"Now get going." He set the pup down and it scrabbled away after its companion.

"You really think you'll make a team of them?" Remi stood up from the hearth, dusting off his hands.

"They're a start. And I have a lot of trapping to do before I can afford a team."

"But them?"

"Why not them?" Spruce stood up and stretched. "There's nothing wrong with them physically, save Sly's blind eye, but—"

"There's a sight more to a good team dog than physical ability. A sight more."

Spruce was staring down at the dogs, tussling half-heartedly on the floor.

"Yeah, there is."

SPRUCE TURNED out to be a decent trapper. He ran the traps along the Tusemuk river and down into the low trees at the foot of the Tanaka range, near Remi's line, and by the time fall came, he had his own cabin, a sled and a couple borrowed dogs for the season, and he made good on every promise and every chance. When he brought in a good load, Timmy Two-Fingers shook his head and said the boy wasn't cut out for this life, no sir, but he still paid him top dollar for the furs. The runts grew to yearlings, and the year after that they were part of a six-dog team, all Spruce's.

IT WAS LATE in the season that it happened—late enough that half the men had come in with the winter's last furs already, and the rest were expected soon. Chegak was the furthest post to the north.

"I can give you fifteen to the pound," Tommy Two-Fingers said, fingering through the furs.

"You paid Reuben sixteen-fifty." Spruce's voice was dry.

"And?"

"These furs are just as good."

"I'll be the judge of that."

"And I can take them elsewhere."

"Where?" Tommy bristled up into Spruce's face.

"Kaquom. There's enough snow falling out there to still make the journey. I could be there and back in a month if the weather holds."

"The weather's not going to hold." Trapper Atka stomped in. "Nasty storm gathering off the coast. That snowfall out there is only getting worse."

Tommy harrumphed in agreement.

Spruce reached up for a bundle of furs and slung them over his shoulder. "Well, I'm in no hurry. Dogs and I have enough to eat. I'll head down to Kaquom when it's over."

"Don't know when it'll be over. This thing's acting like a midwinter storm. Looks like it could blow for weeks."

Tommy whistled long.

"Are you serious?" Spruce turned around. "When is it going to hit?"

"Any day. Some of the fishermen brought word. No one's going down the river or out on the ice to hunt."

Spruce set the furs back down on the counter. "Sixteen-fifty."

"Aha, I have you caught!" crowed Tommy. "It's fifteen, my friend."

"Sixteen-fifty," Spruce repeated, unmoved.

"Hey, Spruce." Reuben Briscoe stomped into the outfitters. "You seen Remi out there?"

"He was a couple days behind me, said he was going to stop at the river camp."

"His team showed up at Halver's without him, their harnesses all chewed through."

"What?"

"Just this past hour. He say anything more?"

"No, he didn't."

"He's a dead man," Atka declared, shaking his head.

"But you know Remi knows the land out there better than anyone," Spruce objected. "Chances are he's holed up and with little or no supplies. Someone gets out there—"

Briscoe put his hands on his hips and shook his head. "That's the trouble. Getting out there. And if he's alive by the time someone gets out there, then he'll have to go along on the sled. And then they'd be fighting their way back in the teeth of the storm."

"I wouldn't go, not in this." Trapper Atka stuck his pipe back in his mouth.

"And no one should." Tommy slammed down his ledger, then added in a gruff tone, "All right, I'll give you sixteen-fifty on 'em."

"It's a sorry thing," said Kaalik, one of the older men of the village, who had been smoking in silence, listening. "Remi was one of the best."

"The land takes its share," intoned Atka, around the stem of his pipe.

"Spruce, I said sixteen-fifty." Tommy raised his voice above the noise of the men's talk. "You taking it or what?"

But Spruce wasn't listening. His shoulders were squared, his chin up, every line in his body tense.

"I'm going."

The room went quiet, the silence as thick as the cigar smoke hanging on the air.

Tommy Two-Fingers broke it with a laugh.

"Son, I'm going to do you a favor right now and tell you to forget it. The winter claims men—it's a fact of life. I've been here since Chegak was settled, and I've seen my share of storms. You won't even make it halfway to the river camp."

"But he's not a fool. Chances are he's holed up."

"I said forget it. That storm's as good as taken him already. Don't let it take you."

"I've been out in storms before."

"Not like this one, son."

"If I go now, chances are decent I can race it out there."

"Even if you made it out there, there's no chance you'd find your way back."

Spruce turned to face the counter. "You have a deal. Sixteen-fifty. My sled's outside. I want it packed. You can subtract it from the total."

"How much?" Tommy was eyeing him grimly, rubbing his beard.

"Supplies for two men, but pack as light as you can. I'm only taking two of the dogs."

WITHIN THE HOUR, Spruce had hitched Sly Eye and Tavii to his sled.

"And what do I do with your stock?" shouted Tommy over the wind.

"I'll be back for it in two weeks. You can have my total waiting. Don't cheat me, now." Spruce tied his scarf over his nose and mouth and fastened his coat up.

"And if you're not back in two weeks?"

Spruce's grim laugh was whisked away by the wind. "I'll be back for it. Hike!"

The dogs shot away and the men stood watching him disappear into the whirling snow.

"Chegak will not be seeing that man again." Kaalik looked to the gnarled gray clouds above and touched his forehead in respect.

THE RIVER CAMP was blown over with snow when Spruce arrived five days later. If there had been evidence of Remi's being there, it was long gone.

The howling of the wind was worsening.

"Remi? Remi!"

Spruce stomped the brake into the deep snow and with a brief "stay" to the dogs, stomped over to the lean-to.

He pried the door open and thrust his head inside. "Remi?"

Leaning against the wall was Remi, bundled in his parka, his head slumped on his chest. At the sound of the voice, he stirred.

Spruce shouldered his way in.

"Remi." He knelt beside him, leaning down to look into his face.

Remi opened his eyes and looked up.

"Spruce? Whatever'd you come back out here for?"

"Find you, of course." Gently Spruce pushed back Remi's hood, regarding the crusted blood from a cut on the side of his head. "Whew. You're lucky."

"Tell me about it. Dragged myself five miles to get here. Been melting snow with my flint and knife, eating leather."

"Lose the dogs?"

"They were a borrowed team." Remi groaned, trying to shift. "They're long gone."

"Yeah, I figure. Look, where are you hurt?"

"Took a fair hit to the head and—my leg's broken."

"Well, you're tough. Figure if you've managed a few days alone, you'll make it a few more."

Remi tried to smile. "Got anything to eat?"

"Sure. Storm's blowing up something awful. I'll bring the things in, we can stay over here a few days, hope this thing blows itself out."

"You're a fool, Spruce."

Spruce grinned. "Sure, Remi."

Four days later, the storm hadn't blown out, and the snow was rising by feet every day. Neither of them was much good at doctoring except for dog ailments, but Spruce managed to splint the leg, and with rest and food, Remi was already looking a little better.

"Don't reckon we can wait much longer," Remi said on the morning of the fourth day.

"Yeah?" Spruce was rubbing Tavii's head in his lap. He had been thinking it, but he knew travel would be rough on Remi.

"It's going to take at least twice as long to get back, and there'll be no hunting."

Spruce continued to stroke Tavii's ears.

"I'll not be holding you up, Spruce. I can go anytime."

"Then I suppose we should move out as soon as we can." Spruce got up, shifting Tavii. "I'll go get the sled ready."

Neither of them had to say it—they both knew their chances were slim even now, but if they waited, they'd be slimmer.

By midmorning, they had left the lean-to behind, gone in the shrieking wind.

. . .

THEY WERE only hours into their trek before the reality of the situation hit. The wind was bad, slinging hard snow in their faces, and the dogs were using all their energy fighting the wind. With his leg, there was nothing Remi could do but ride in the sled basket, which left little room for supplies, and Spruce had to walk behind the runners to conserve the dogs' energy.

It had been five days to the river camp in moderately ill weather, running with the wind, not against it. The way ahead now was gained by inches. Around midafternoon, by Remi's watch, they stopped for a rest, and Spruce gave the dogs some water from a canteen he kept in his coat. Remi took only a swig of spirits from a flask in his coat and said he wasn't hungry.

They continued, inching their way forward, playing the wind, going along the side of it, cutting through, and then going along its side again.

The dogs stopped short. Sly Eye began to sniff the ground.

"Come on, Sly!" Spruce shouted. "Come on!"

Sly wagged his tail and sniffed the ground but didn't budge.

"All right, I'll see what it is."

"Following the river, it's liable to be an overflow," said Remi, shading his eyes, peering through the stinging snow. Spruce waded up to them through the snow and tested the ground in front of them. Water with no immediate bottom met his boot and he withdrew it quickly. The trouble with following the river home was that this late in the season the ice wasn't stable to run on, and it created deep overflows.

He tested the ground in front of them twenty feet in either direction. All deep water.

"Come on, Sly, Tavii!" He whistled, and the dogs followed after him as he veered sharply left. If they headed inland a little, chances were they'd find a dry patch before too long.

Another twenty feet down, he found a spot and gave the lead back to the dogs. If he gave them the word, they'd find the safest path on their own.

"Mean storm," he said, leaning close to Remi.

Remi laughed. "Bloody right."

They dodged overflows the rest of the day, Spruce stopping every so often to dry the dogs' paws if they crossed a shallow one. The next day was the same, crawling in the teeth of the wind and avoiding and crossing overflows, barely making headway.

It was close to noon by the color of the gray storm, and three times already they had been forced to stop to make sure the dogs were dry. Spruce had taken half his clothes off more than once in order to keep them dry, but despite every precaution, his mittens were soaked through on the last pass.

He stripped them off with a muttered oath, throwing them in the front of the sled.

"Take mine," Remi said, pulling his off and holding them out. "My hands haven't much to do right now.

"Thanks, old man."

Spruce took the mittens and went to pull them on.

"No, no, no—" Spruce held up an unsteady hand. Two fingers were white and waxy. Not just the tips, but most of the way down. He bit off an oath.

He began to unbutton his coat and shirt to thrust his

hand inside, but stopped. In such cases, he would normally hurry back to his lean-to, build a fire, warm them up. But here they were, midday, in the swirling storm, weaving between overflows.

The dogs had to come first. He pulled his hand out and stuck it into his mitten. Chances were they were going to run into more water, and to warm it just to freeze it again was more dangerous than leaving it be.

At least, right now, they didn't hurt. He waded up to the front of the sled and checked the harnesses again. He couldn't risk losing the dogs right now.

"Ayyup!" The wind stole the frosty breath right out of his mouth.

THE FOOD WAS RUNNING LOW. Spruce drew his knife and made another notch in the side of his sled,

counting silently the marks he had made since they had left the river cabin. Seventeen. He counted backwards. Twenty-one days of a storm. Trapper Atka had meant what he said.

"Come on, Remi. I've dug a shelter. Let's get some food." The leg was a bit better, but Remi himself was worse. He had been running a low fever for days, and it was hard to get him to eat anything. He was not nearly as tall as Spruce, but easily twice his size through the shoulders, and it was always a trial to get him out of the sled and into a shelter with his leg.

"The victuals have to be running low," said Remi, once he was settled inside the shelter and Spruce was bent over the branches he had cut from a nearby pine.

"Yeah, but let me worry about that." Spruce kept his back to him. "We still have some."

"And do you know where we are?"

"I figure we're getting closer."

"Still on the river?"

"More or less."

This was the third time today Remi had asked. Spruce glanced over his shoulder. It was always hard to see color in Remi's cold-hardened face, but his sunken cheeks were clear. The truth was, between his sweat and Remi's knowledge, he had stretched the time as long as he could. But under nine feet of snow, the landmarks were changed.

He opened the bag of food and pulled out a fistful of dried berries and the bark he had stripped from a tree they'd passed the day before. Tonight was all wild snow and howling wind.

"Eat up." He handed over all the berries and half of the bark and went to the front of the shelter. Tavii and Sly Eye were eating outside.

A deep, throaty howl cut through the noise of the wind. Spruce started up. Sly Eye was on his feet, bristling, Tavii beside him, every line in her body taut.

"Easy now." Spruce reached for his rifle and crawled up through the entrance of the shelter.

Tavii slunk back to him at his voice.

Another howl broke the wind. Tavii began to bark furiously, her voice joining Sly's. She was shaking, pressed against Spruce's legs.

Another howl and behind him, Remi swore.

"You watch those bullets, son, or we're dead. Those aren't timber wolves, they're black ones."

Spruce had only heard rumors of them, the black

wolves that ran in the Tanakas, but he knew from the howl that these weren't the same wolves he had become accustomed to along the river. Something must have driven them down into the lowlands.

"Does fire hold them?"

"A big one does."

Their fire was not a big one. With a team of six or seven dogs, wolves didn't often bother, but there were only two here, and two injured men. Wolves had a sixth sense for weakness.

He had only two shots in his rifle. He needed more. He braced himself and ran for the sled, out into the dark.

"Where you do you think you're going, boy?"

He ignored Remi's voice. Tavii trotted behind, moving on stiffened legs, her nose in the air. She was still afraid, but if he was going out, so was she.

He seized the handlebars of the sled and dragged it backward, toward the entrance, with all his might. If he could partially block the entrance, they'd have a better chance.

Then he saw a flash of green eyes in the firelight. He whipped his gun to his shoulder and fired.

Tavii shrank against him at the sound and he seized the sled again, wrenching it through the snow after him.

Close enough. He dug into the bottom of the sled, half spilling the bullets. Sly Eye was still out in the wind where the sled had been, barking his defiance.

"Sly, get!" He whistled, sharp, and the dog came around behind the sled, barking from his new position.

A pair of eyes appeared just beyond them. Spruce raised the rifle and shot.

He was reloading as quickly as he could with his frozen fingers when Remi's voice arrested him. "Spruce!"

He glanced up to see a wolf the size of a small horse advancing. Sly and Tavii barked wildly, their backs standing like bristle brushes. He was no stranger to loading a gun while facing death, but his heart still pounded in his ears. Even years of practice cannot take that away.

He whipped the rifle back up to his shoulder and emptied both barrels into the beast. It fell with a great cry, then a slow wheeze.

The howls started up again, fierce, but a little further away. The dogs barked themselves hoarse, keeping it up until the howls were gone.

Tavii shoved her nose against Spruce's elbow and whined.

"Good dogs." He lowered the rifle.

There was an awful crackling sound from his fingers, and the stock of the rifle fell from his hand into the snow.

That couldn't be good.

He pulled the mitten off slowly and winced. A foul smell rose immediately from the blistered, black fingers. Had he been home, able to rest and keep them dry, chances were the black would have sloughed off in time and the skin grown back fresh. But this was gangrene. He'd seen it before many times—times he wanted to forget forever. The smell alone made bile rise in his throat.

He turned to look at Remi, but his friend was already asleep, head slumped on his chest, even after the excitement of the wolves.

Remi was sleeping too much. Nowadays he did little else but sleep and eat the rations Spruce forced on him.

He cut a strip from his blanket to wrap the fingers in

and let it be. In another day or two, he'd have to make a decision. Tonight, he kept watch.

BY MORNING he could feel the damp prickle of fever coming over him, and there were red streaks working their way up from the base of the fingers into his hand.

By evening, he had made up his mind.

It was impossible to tell how far they were from Chegak. Nothing was visible in the storm, and even with his help, the dogs could barely make headway against the wind.

He couldn't risk it. Another day of this and it would be too late for him. The fingers had to come off.

He bedded the dogs down, dug a snow shelter, and got Remi settled.

He pressed his good hand against Remi's head. Still fevered. It was the cold, the lack of food, the leg, and the head. Take one of those out and he might hold his own right enough, but as it was, his stubborn strength was the only reason he wasn't already with the beyond. And Spruce didn't know how much longer that would last against a storm like this.

The wind howled cruelly outside. The dogs were curled up in the snow, tight little balls of fur. He got out his knife and started to sharpen it.

"Blunt it already, Spruce?" Remi was awake again. His voice was unsteady, even as he joked.

Spruce threw a smile over his shoulder and kept at it. He sharpened the blade until it was razor keen and forced himself to stop there. It was a thing best done quickly, before a man had time to think.

"Hey, Remi, you got anything more in that flask?"

"A little. You feeling the nip tonight?"

"Yeah." Remi dug in his pocket feebly and held out the flask. For a moment Spruce's heart almost failed him, but seeing Remi like this—weak and making jokes to lighten their situation, though he had been born and raised in the wilds and knew their danger better than anyone—well, it gave him strength. If he sickened and died, he'd let them all down.

Spruce grasped the flask and took a long swig. The spirits burned all the way down, and he handed it back before Remi could say anything.

He tramped out to the sled, his back to Remi so he couldn't see what he was doing. He tore a strip of clean canvas from one of the stays and pinned it under his knee so it wouldn't fly away in the wind. He took his belt off and tightened it across the palm of his hand as hard as he could.

Then he gripped the edge of the sled, gritted his teeth, and did it.

A harsh gasp tore itself out of his chest as he finished and Tavii started up, her ears perked.

"Spruce!" Remi's voice came from the shelter. "What happened?"

Spruce clutched his hand, breathless, his jaw clenched, biting back any sound.

"Spruce?"

"It's nothing," he managed, the two words all he could get out. He swallowed, pressed his forehead to his gripped hands. "I'm fine."

He reached for the bandage and clenched his teeth as he bound up the bleeding stumps. Tavii came over and sniffed his face as if to make sure he wasn't dying, but he couldn't speak, even to reassure her. She drew her own conclusion after a moment and let him be. After a few minutes of fumbling, he managed to get it bandaged well enough to stanch the bleeding, and then he sheathed his knife with trembling hands.

His head was swimming. He stood up to go in, and the world went black.

He woke on the ground with the dogs licking his face. Everything felt numb except his hand, which burned with pain. He stumbled back to the shelter, wrapped himself in a blanket, and closed his eyes. Right before he drifted off, he felt a hesitant nose creep under one arm, then a long sigh as Tavii laid down against him.

Morning dawned in colors, and it took Spruce a moment in his dazed state to realize why he felt relief.

The storm had broken. There was actually a dawn outside.

Remi was still asleep, so Spruce pulled the mitten off and examined the wrapping. Some blood had leaked through and he could feel the heat throbbing through it, but the streaks hadn't moved past his wrist. He let out his breath and slumped back against the firm wall of the shelter.

Tavii yawned beside him and got stiffly to her feet.

"It's going to be a little harder to take care you like this, girl." He rubbed the muscle above her shoulder with his good hand. She gave him a lolling grin and sat back on her haunches. At least she didn't seem to care.

He got up and she trotted after him. The sun glared off the snow blindingly, and he shaded his eyes and squinted.

They had a chance. Last night, feverish with pain, he

had begun to let despair creep in. But he could see now. The river wound westward like a snake, and the trees pointed the way to the coast.

"Remi—" He ducked back into the shelter. "We're going home."

NIGHTFALL CAME, and Spruce set up camp. His head and eyes ached, and it was slow work with his raw hand, but they had made progress today. Real progress. Another storm was gathering on the horizon, but if they could put in one more good day before it hit, they had a fighting chance.

He helped Remi into the shelter. The man was feverish again, hotter than before. His stomach sank. If the weather held, maybe they'd make it in time.

"Come on, Remi," he said, mustering up a cheerful tone. "Not much longer now. Let's eat."

A DOG-NOSE, shoved into his face, woke him.

"Easy, easy, what is it?" He squinted at the darkness. His eyes hurt something terrible, but he couldn't hear anything amiss.

The fire had gone out.

He reached into the pocket of his coat and struck a match. Nothing. He heard it strike, he could feel the heat against his fingers, but it was still dark as night.

A cold chill ran over him as he shook the match out.

He moved slowly to where Remi lay and shook his shoulder gently.

"Remi? Remi, listen, I—" He stopped to listen, trying to hear if Remi's breathing had changed or if he stirred.

"I'm listening, boy."

"I think I'm snow-blind. Is—is it bright out?"

"Powerful bright."

There was dead silence between them.

"Now there, don't look so crushed." Remi's voice was like sled runners over gravel. "Give it a day or two, it may come back."

"We don't have a day or two, Remi." He didn't want to say what he knew—that he was burning with fever too, that he had been giving Remi all the food for the last two days, that if he laid down to sleep, he didn't know if he'd even wake up again.

With an unsteady hand he pulled the scrap of cloth he wore around his throat off and rolled it tightly, binding it awkwardly over his eyes to protect them from the light he knew was there but could not see.

"Spruce...."

He swallowed the lump in his throat. "Yeah?"

"It's not your fault." Remi's voice was dry, weak. He wished he could see the man. He could know better how he was if he could see.

"If I could see, we could leave."

"Spruce, you did what you could. Sometimes the wilds win." A rattling breath.

"But I don't want to give up."

"Think of the dogs...." His voice trailed off.

"Remi?" No answer.

He reached in, pulling the blanket and the coat back, and pressed his ear to the man's chest. The barest flutter met his ear.

"Remi," he said gently, steeling himself, "you have to answer me."

Nothing.

"Remi, you have to answer me. It's important."

Still nothing.

He replaced the blanket slowly. Yesterday he had been so full of hope. But that's the way it was in nature, wasn't it? The way a man looked well and whole in the moments before his death.

And now death had come for its due.

He crawled out to the sled, feeling his way carefully across the icy snow. He could hear the dogs perk up and shake themselves off as he came out.

They had been everything to him. His last kindness would be his death sentence.

But no—he was dead already. He'd been brave but a fool to dare death like this, and Tommy Two-Fingers was right.

He wasn't coming back.

He felt his way up the harness, unbuckled first Tavii and then Sly Eye. Tavii immediately reached up and licked his burning face.

He pulled her silky ears gently. "I'm sorry, Tavii, Sly Eye. It's the end of the trail for me. I wish I could do different."

Her tail thumped pleasantly.

"You were good dogs, you hear me? Good dogs." He pressed his face against Sly's muzzle and then against Tavii's. "It's time you go on now. I can't feed you and you can't pull us." His voice cracked. "But you tried. You did your very best. Go on now," he urged gently.

Tavii panted into his face expectantly.

"I said go on!" He waved his hand. She ran a distance and doubled back. He could hear her panting, waiting on him.

He stood up, his head feeling like it weighed a hundred pounds.

"Go on!" Still the uncertain dancing of paws on the hard snow. "You hear me? Go! Don't make me yell at you anymore!" Tears stung his already aching eyes.

He limped back to the sled basket, pulled out his rifle. "I said, get!"

He shouted with all the breath left in his lungs and fired a shot into the frozen air.

The sideways skitter of Tavii's paws at the sound of the gunshot cut through him like a knife. He steeled himself and emptied the other barrel.

"Go on! Get lost! You hear me?"

The distant sound of running.

He lowered the gun and drew the back of his bandaged hand beneath his numb nose. There was three weeks' scrap of beard on his face, and this last week it was like it quit trying.

He slumped against the sled. It was sunny here, sunny for a few hours more. The storm would cover them, perhaps only a matter of miles from safety, and someone would find them when the thaw came.

But at least—at least dying of cold was gentler than a bullet, gentler than the pain in his hand. It would be a good thing, a good thing to sleep....

THE GENTLE CRUNCH of paws on the ice-crusted snow broke through the thick fog in his head. The sound was, for a moment, swept away by a gust of wind, but came again as the wind subsided. It was cold again, the warmth of the sun gone.

The warm, limp body of a hare, by the feel of the coat, was thrust into his face. He smelled the sharp tang of hot blood. Sly Eye—he knew by the stiff hair that rubbed against his cheek—whined and began to lick his face.

He dragged himself up, his head thundering. He took hold of the dog and began to sob into his neck. They were supposed to go fend for themselves, and instead they brought him food, food they certainly wanted themselves. Sly Eye wriggled from his grasp and began to lick his face again. A thin whine and the crunch of snow behind him betrayed Tavii's presence.

"You were supposed to leave," he whispered, shoving the blindfold up to wipe his eyes. "You *wukuk* fools, you were supposed to leave." Sly's tail thudded against his leg. He was panting, the sort that Spruce knew to be his tongue-out, grinning pant.

He felt over the limp body, his fingers sticking only in one spot along the hare's throat.

The dogs hadn't eaten any of it.

Tears stung his eyes as he pressed his face into Sly's, and then Tavii's, as she thrust her thin nose between them.

"Thank you, you stupid, loyal fools."

Tavii backed up, her whole body quivering at the praise in his voice.

He reached up with his good hand and pulled himself to his knees beside the sled basket. Then he crawled back to the shelter, the still-warm rabbit in his hand.

"Remi—Remi." He propped himself against the wall beside his friend and pried his mouth open. He dipped his fingers into the warm blood and let the blood drip into Remi's mouth.

After a moment, he felt his throat swallow.

Again and again he dipped his fingers into the blood and pressed it to Remi's mouth, waiting each time to make sure he swallowed.

At last he wiped his fingers on his coat and covered Remi again with the furs.

He sat in the shelter of the sled and tore pieces from the hare with his knife, sharing it equally between himself and the dogs.

Hunger roared over his body, almost beating out the fever in his head and his limbs. It was a mistake, eating. Death would come so much harder now, after a taste of hope.

But the dogs deserved for him to try.

He put it off a few minutes more, dragged Remi out to the sled, bundled him up. It took painfully long with his fevered hand and without the help of his eyes, but he did it.

Then he called the dogs, kneeling beside them.

Tears ran hot down his unfeeling cheeks, freezing halfway down his face. He reached out and felt their heads, Sly Eye's wiry fur, the silky spot on top of Tavii's head.

"I'm sorry," he choked. The air through his scarf shattered each breath as it hit his lungs. "I'm sorry I can't do anything more."

Sly Eye thrust his nose into his face, the touch cold and reassuring, then licked him between the eyes.

"I'm sorry, my friend." He rubbed Sly behind the ears a little harder. Tavii whined in her throat. He could hear her feet shifting uneasily on the icy snow, doing the little restless dance they always did when she wanted so badly to help and didn't know what to do.

He reached out and wrapped his arms around her neck, drawing her to his chest, kissing her on the head through his frost-caked scarf. Her tail thudded against his leg.

It was over, but they were not ready to give up. He owed it to them to fight to the last second of life. He could die, but he couldn't quit on them.

The wind blew cold and tense, blowing Tavii's coat the wrong way, pushing the fur of his hood against his unseeing eyes.

A storm was coming.

He put them in double lead, pulled off his mittens to feel every line and buckle to make sure they were secure.

Then he knelt before them, feeling their faces for the very last time.

"Home, Tavii. Home, Sly."

WHEN TOMMY TWO-FINGERS looked out his storefront window on the morning of the fifteenth, a week after the blizzard ended, he saw two limping dogs, tracking blood through bound-up feet, dragging a sled with a man slumped over the handlebars.

His broom clattered to the floor as he ran out into the bone-shattering cold in only his shirt.

The dogs didn't even look his way or perk their ears. They merely came to a halt and laid down in the dirty snow.

"Is—is this Chegak?" The man, a wasted figure, spoke. They were Spruce's dogs, and it was Spruce's voice.

"Yes, it's Chegak—by thunder, we thought you were dead!" A crowd was gathering around the sled.

"He's in here, Remi's in here."

"By gur, he's still alive!" Hands reached for the man in the sled, lifting him out, running him to the warmth of the outfitters.

Stiff, half-crawling, Spruce felt his way over the sled, up to the dogs.

"Easy now, don't worry about them, we'll take good care of them."

He didn't answer, kept feeling his way along with his hands.

"He's stone blind!" called one man. "Man's blind as midnight!" Hands reached to stop him, voices urging him in a tangle to get inside, he was sick, he was in no condition to be out here, he had to get warm immediately.

He shook them all off.

He knelt shakily in front of the weary dogs who lay with their heads on their paws. Pulled off his mittens, showing blackened fingertips and the raw stumps where two fingers should be.

His frost-blistered face pressed against their cold, weary muzzles, his voice so low it was little more than a moan.

"Good dogs."

He collapsed to the gray snow.

THE IMPOSSIBLE LUCK OF EPIRVIKK HEFT

OR

HOW MR. STONE WON A WAGER

6

THE IMPOSSIBLE LUCK OF EPIRVIKK HEFT

The sturdy door of Stone's trading post ground open, dragging with it a quantity of ice and dirty snow. Heavy boots kicked off the snow against the doorjamb and strode slowly forward.

The chatter died, silence hanging as thick as the cigar smoke. Eyes went to the figure of the newcomer and glanced away just as quickly.

Epirvikk Heft was a man of moderate height, with brown hair that curled a little and a scrap of a beard, but he walked like a soldier: quiet authority and a hint of the dangerous. The general opinion in town was that Heft was as mysterious as they came. After all, he had one native name and one foreign, he wore a patch over one eye, he ran the best trapline in four hundred miles, and—most mystifying of all—he was in business with Mr. Erasmus Stone.

He stopped before the counter. "Stone?"

There was a low, swift murmur, and a couple of the wiser men finished their drinks and slipped out the side door.

Heft and Stone were a joke in Kaquom. With Mr. Stone being rather short and gray and round and Heft being so terribly serious, the humor of their names injected itself without much help from already irreverent minds. If he had known, Mr. Stone might even have chuckled at the idea. But no one would dare so much as whisper a joke around Heft, unless they were drunk.

Stone hurried into the room, a pencil behind one ear, drying his hands on a dirty old rag.

"Oh, Heft, Heft—it is good to see you!" He threw out his hands in greeting. "Most of all because I know the wolves didn't get you this time."

Heft's laugh was little more than a short grunt.

"Have a seat, do."

Heft shoved the hood of his parka back, pulled his fur mitts off, and slapped them onto the counter.

The few men still left at the counter (which doubled as a bar during the day, when Stone was not available to host at the more commodious Pick and Collarbone) slid their drinks off and retreated to the far tables.

"It will be one moment. I will pull out our best," Stone promised, disappearing into the dingy room behind the counter.

Heft raised his voice to be heard in the back room. "They said you wanted to talk to me."

"Who said?"

"The boys in the dog lot."

"The boys in the dog lot…."

Stone muttered and kept on muttering under his breath.

"So." Heft drew the word out slowly.

"What do you mean by 'so'?" asked Stone, setting down a dusty bottle and rifling on his person for a corkscrew.

"So what do you want to talk to me about?"

"Oh—did I say I did?"

"Enough." Heft shook his head and took a drink from the glass set in front of his knuckles.

He sucked in a sudden deep breath through his teeth. "Whe-eew, Stone, this is nasty. Why on earth are you serving it? You'll give us a bad name."

"My dear Mr. Heft." Stone stumped over, seizing the small glass from his partner's fingers. "That is not for you —*this* is the good stuff." He pushed over an empty glass and poured out a mouthful from the freshly opened dusty bottle. "And when you're the only name—" he tapped the side of his nose conspiratorially— "it doesn't matter what sort of stuff it is."

Heft retained a stubborn silence and raised the new glass hesitantly to his lips.

Stone lifted his own glass. "To another successful run."

Heft hesitated.

"It—it was successful?" asked Stone, suddenly worried.

"Of course. But I don't like your manner."

"Me, have a manner?" Stone gave a disbelieving chuckle. "Don't you worry about that. To success."

This time, they both drank.

"You had better hurry it up." Heft set his glass down with a hard thunk. "I have to unload my sled, and I would rather do it before dark."

"Well, well," began Stone decidedly. "I have been thinking, and I have had an idea."

"Stone, no." Heft pushed back the stool and stood up. "Not another idea. I mean it—"

"Just hear me out, hear me out," protested Stone.

"No, I've had enough. I mean it this time."

"But you haven't even heard my idea. It's very good."

"You have one minute to convince me it is worth my time."

"Now, Heft, you know that isn't fair…listen, I think we ought to organize a dogsled race—between the dog-drivers, we could put together a purse, and then run bets through the trading post."

"Well, it's not the worst idea you have had." Heft leaned his arms forward onto the counter.

"Taking all comers, but touted as a match race," continued Stone, encouraged. "Between you and Grim Halver."

"Grim Halver?" At the sound of Heft's raised voice, the few customers still left fell perfectly silent and moved toward the door.

"Have you taken leave of your senses? My dogs are fast, but not faster than Halver's. I guarantee it."

"Come on, then—don't be so hard on yourself."

"I am not being hard on myself. I am being realistic." Heft snatched up his mittens.

"It's too late," Stone said in a sad, resigned voice. "I've already done it."

Heft stopped mid-stride. "Done it? Done what?"

"Entered you into the stakes."

The thunderous crash upon the counter made the glasses rattle. Three swift strides from heavy boots sounded, and the door opened and slammed.

"I say," remarked Stone to the empty room. "He took that uncommon well."

. . .

Heft stood on the low row of logs that served as a porch before the door of the trading post, staring out at the empty, churned-snow street.

"Fool!" he burst out, to no one in particular. He shoved his mittens into the wide pocket of his parka and stepped down into the street, headed for the dog lot.

His team was settled quietly in the snow, a couple of the dogs uncurling themselves and stretching as he approached.

"Evening, Mr. Heft!" The voice was young and bright—a local lad, the one he usually paid to help him unload the goods at the trading post.

"Evening."

"Are we going to unload tonight?" The lad glanced at the thick line of light on the darkening horizon.

"Not tonight." Heft gave one contemptuous glance back in the direction of the trading post. "In the morning, at first light. Now go on."

The boy gave a nod of thanks and ran off, eager to be away from Heft's ill mood.

Heft went to his sled and dragged it over the last few yards into the shed that stood behind the trading post. He pulled a satchel of his own things out, throwing the strap over his shoulder. He untied his leader—a strong, wolfish dog with a blue-black coat and white markings—and with a brief "Come," strode off toward the edge of town.

East of town stood a small cabin, snow-drifted and dark. He pushed in through the door, and stood a moment in the dim, dusty silence. It was his place: a poor excuse for a home, but he didn't stay put much. A low wooden bed was nailed to the floor, a pile of cut wood sat against one wall, and the hearth had ashes in it from some traveler who had helped himself on a cold night likely three months past.

The dog settled on his haunches in the doorway.

Heft cleaned out the ashes, stacked the wood in the hearth, and struck a flint. When the fire had been nursed to a strong, crackling flame, he got up and went to a cupboard in the wall, taking down two blankets and a fur.

"Come," he urged the dog, who immediately thumped his tail and trotted into the cabin.

Heft bolted the door, spread the fur down before the fire, and took jerky and *muktuk* out of his pack. His dog settled on the floor beside him with a yawn and a groan.

"Fool," he muttered again, to himself.

The dog perked up with a low whine and he reached out, running his hand over the dog's ears.

"Good boy."

He ate in silence, staring into the flame.

THE NEXT DAY, Grim Halver came to Kaquom. Morning was still pale, and Heft was in the middle of unloading his furs, an assortment of trappers and dog-drivers loitering near at hand to gauge his success.

Reuben Briscoe lounged against the doorframe, eyeing the thick martin and fox plews. "Those are some thick pelts," he remarked, moving aside for Heft to come past with a stack of the furs over one shoulder.

Briscoe leaned in through the door, calling after him, "You get them out Tusemuk way?" His nearest companion pulled at his sleeve and shook his head. Everyone knew not to bother asking Heft where he trapped. He never did give an answer.

A chorus of barks on the edge of town heralded a newcomer.

A single sled with nine dogs in harness swung around the corner of the furthest buildings, roaring like an avalanche down main street.

The idle men all perked up and stomped out of their warm corners to watch his arrival. Even Heft paused for a brief moment as he pulled another bundle of furs from his sled and looked up as the team pulled to a halt before the trading post.

Grim Halver was a pale man, as if the frost had crept into his face and hair and stayed there permanently. He walked around the front of the team to his leaders, slowly pulling the gloves from his hands.

"Welcome to Kaquom!" greeted one of the old-timers, trudging through the thick snow and giving a low nod in greeting.

Halver returned it respectfully, though his air remained distant.

"What do you think of him?" asked Reuben, folding his arms.

"Arrogant." Heft shouldered the bundle. "But he can afford to be."

"Is there a place for my dogs?" Halver asked the general assemblage. "A little removed from the dog lot, perhaps?"

A boy was sent ahead to show the way. Halver's gaze went to Heft, still unloading the sled, his dogs rubbing themselves in the snow.

"Hmm."

Heft raised his gaze briefly from his last bundle and met the appraising gaze stonily.

Halver gave a brief, flat smile and, his eyes still on Heft's dogs, called his own up.

They shot away in a spray of snow.

Reuben gave a long whistle. "That's dog for you. I'd like to get one chance at that kind of bloodline."

Heft stomped his sled hook into the icy snow and shouldered past Briscoe with the last of the furs, shoving the door closed with his foot.

Stone had his large ledger book out and his spectacles on his nose, peering at the lines.

Heft set the bundle down with a thump. "That's the last of it."

Stone looked up, still counting the bundles, tallying them.

"Good—good, good," he replied absently.

Heft leaned forward, pressing his fists into the counter. "And now a word."

Stone adjusted his glasses and looked up, his pen pausing on the paper. "Right now? Can't I finish the figures?"

"No, now. I can tell you the figures straight from my head if you forget. Now listen. This is very important, Stone. How much money of ours did you tie up in this race? Briscoe told me there was a substantial purse."

Stone fidgeted a little, running up figures in his head, muttering to himself.

"Stone, do not put me off. You don't need to figure the amount. How much of our money is tied up in this race?"

"Briscoe shouldn't talk so much."

"Briscoe is only repeating what all of Kaquom already knows. How much of our money is in this race?"

"A bit," Stone admitted.

"A figure, please."

"Three thousand?"

The sum hit Heft like a blow across the face and it was

a moment before he could even speak. When he did, his voice was still, like ice on a lake. He was furious.

"This is why you cannot involve me without warning in every hare-brained scheme you have. I must have a say."

"But isn't that what partnership is?" Stone looked plaintively up from his ledger, blowing on the pages and shutting it. "You have to trust me at least a little, Heft, or we'll never get anywhere."

"You either don't understand or you won't! Halver's dogs are faster than mine, plain and simple. We are going to lose every cent we put into this race."

Stone finished wiping the counter industriously and threw the towel over his shoulder. "You just leave that to me."

"What do you mean, 'leave that to me'? The dogs are mine—I know what they are capable of, and they are not capable of beating Halver in the race."

There was a silence between them.

"And I am not going to cheat," he added grimly.

"Who said anything about cheating?" asked Stone brightly. Too brightly, perhaps.

"I mean it. I'll walk out of this race if you do."

"No, you won't," said Stone, attempting to be firm. "You must at least give us a chance to get the money back."

"You cheat and I cut out of that race, three thousand or no."

"You always know best," replied Stone with a shrug that suggested the opposite.

Heft dragged his boot off the rung of the stool beside him with a dark, weary look. "If I always knew best, I wouldn't have gone into business with you in the first place."

. . .

The Pick and Collarbone was full that night. Full of unwashed fishermen and out-of-luck miners, full of laughter urged on by whiskey, full of pipe and cigar smoke that hung about the low ceiling and the yellow lamps.

Stone was supplying the drink and the talk, brewing a fever of excitement, crowding out every worry of winter and every tightened belt, leaving only room for the race and the dogs.

Reuben Briscoe was holding court at the bar, outlining why one man or another had the better chance of winning the race. His points tended strongly toward Halver.

Heft sat in a corner by himself, an invisible line drawn between him and the rest of the rowdy room.

"Sure, Heft knows the land around here all right," said Briscoe. "But if you haven't got the speed, it's not much advantage."

"That's the thing." Halver tilted his chair back until it creaked. "Heft's dogs won't see mine after the start. We'll be a line on the horizon."

"What about Briscoe's?" called a man from the bar.

Raucous laughter. Everyone knew that Briscoe was running as the dark horse, on the off-chance the two fron-trunners took each other out.

"My dogs have made the run from Chegak to Kaquom in a week and a half," Briscoe pronounced over the clamor. "What say you to that?"

Impressed whistles and shouts of "liar" met this boast.

"A wager!" Halver lifted his small glass high. "That my dogs beat Heft's by a quarter of the course!"

An appreciative roar from the crowd.

"I'll wager five to one it's so."

"And if it's not?" another rowdy miner spoke up.

Halver smiled knowingly. "As I said, I'm wagering five to one on it. Five to one that Heft's dogs don't have it in them."

Heft seemed deaf to the talk, his fist around a worn old glass in his dark corner, as if he wasn't half owner of the Pick and Collarbone.

"What says he to that?"

A lull ensued as the others waited for Heft to take the bait.

"Come on, Heft!" urged Briscoe. "What say you?"

"Putting a rival down is for the weak." Heft touched his lips to the whiskey in his glass. "I'll not indulge in it."

"But he's right there. Hungry for it. He's waiting for you to say something."

A glance proved this true. Halver was sipping a brandy, one heavy boot up on the chair opposite, his frosty eyes watching Heft with a touch of laughter in them.

"I said I'll not do it," said Heft, a touch of annoyance in his voice.

"Now, man—he'll think you mean it badly!"

Heft's frosty eye fixed Briscoe like a spear. "Let him."

Briscoe conceded defeat and went back to the bar for a watered whiskey.

But Halver pressed on.

"Come now, Epirvikk!" he called out in a clear, ringing voice. "Have you nothing to say? A true dog-man never allows his team to be so ill-used."

Heft opened his mouth as if rolling a reply around on his tongue, then swung his shoulders away.

Halver laughed. Being an outsider, he was not familiar

with the local convention that forbade laughing at Heft. A few others who had reached their limit for the night joined in.

Epirvikk Heft rose from his table, knocking the chair over. "I'll say one thing, and one thing only." His voice was deep and slow. "The man who boasts too long will one day outboast himself.

Halver rose to meet him, a thin, expectant smile on his face. "And the one who is threatened by a mere boast has lost already."

They stood like men carved of ice, eye to eye, neither moving.

"Oh, my dear gentlemen!" Stone hurried over, smacking his hands on his worn apron. "There's no call for a fight. Look, Mr. Halver, I say, let's look over the course, shall we?"

"Doesn't he need to as well?" Halver didn't shift his gaze.

"That's my advantage," said Heft. "I know every stone of this area."

He stalked out into the night.

KAQUOM WAS abuzz with the excitement of the race. It was to be run at midday, which afforded the men a whole morning to make bets, look over the dogs, and get into arguments about the teams and drivers.

Halver stood with the others outside the outfitters, discussing the course, discussing the bets, seeming in fine spirits.

Heft did not make an appearance until less than an hour before the race, when he came out to harness his dogs.

One of the hangers-on fell in step beside him as he strode across the frozen ground to the dog lot. "Halver's wagered all of his earnings from this year."

"Interesting." Heft kept walking.

"Is that all you have to say?"

Heft swung around to fix him with his eye. "What do you want me to say?"

"What you think of Halver?"

Heft turned abruptly and continued towards the dog lot.

"Do you know what he's been saying about you and your dogs all morning?"

"I do not know and I do not care."

Heft's sled had been dragged out to the lot for him and he waved off all the young village boys milling around asking to help.

One by one he hitched the dogs up, checking their feet carefully. He drove them out to the street where a crowd had already gathered.

Heft let his breath out in a disapproving whistle and trudged up to the front of the team. He knelt down in the snow beside his leader. "Well, lad, all I can ask is what you can give."

The dog reached up and licked him appreciatively.

"Good boy."

He straightened, pulled his gloves back on, and nearly ran into Stone, who had come up behind him. "What do you want?"

"Just to wish you luck."

"Hmm."

This time the innocent look on Stone's face appeared genuine. "Promise me one thing—don't give up."

"Hadn't any intention of that," Heft retorted. "Now that you've gotten me stuck in this tomfool race, I am going to try to win—maybe keep us from losing all our money."

"Good. Very good." Stone tapped the side of his nose. "Good indeed."

"What?"

"Mister Heft, where do you shoot to kill a *nanuk*?"

"What are you doing?"

"Just answer my question, please."

"Best place, if you can get it, is in the ear."

"Right. Because if you shot his flank or his leg or his side, you'd be dead before you got three rounds in," said Stone.

"And?" He was nervous, if Heft could ever be called nervous. Adjusting his gloves, checking his grip on the handlebars, tugging at the leftover bit on the rawhide he had used to wrap them.

"It's all in knowing where to shoot," smiled Stone. "Good luck."

And he was gone, stumping away down the street through the dirty snow. Heft shook his head grimly. Either he was *wukuk* or Stone was. Maybe both.

Halver's team arrived last, breezing up to the line with the ease of a seal in water.

One of the old-timers held his shotgun aloft, his finger on the trigger. "Are we ready, gentlemen?"

If anyone had an answer, it was drowned out by the cheers of the bystanders.

The gunshot split the air and they were off.

. . .

THE SNOW SKIMMED hard beneath the feet of his dogs. The town and then the trees whipped past. Halver was already ahead. His team had been almost silent, their feet and their breath the only thing that gave their presence away as they glided past, turned around a formation of rocks, and disappeared from sight.

"There goes your three thousand, Stone," Heft had muttered under his breath.

The whole course through, he never saw Halver again.

The only excitement was a near-tangle at the turnoff to a risky shortcut that Briscoe was trying to take at the same time Heft was trying to turn onto the slightly longer but much more dependable path. After that, the trail was clear and his dogs settled into a mile-eating run.

It was not until he was rounding the last turn before town that he spied another team, slim and loud, on the adjacent trail.

Briscoe, coming off that shortcut. Proof that shortcuts don't always work.

He might not be able to beat the likes of Grim Halver, but he was not going to finish behind the likes of Reuben Briscoe. Heft stepped off the runners and began to run with the dogs.

"Come on!" he bellowed. "That's it, Wolf! Hike! Onward!"

His leader rose to the challenge. The dogs came alive, straining into their harnesses, giving him a pace he had never seen from them before.

A second place purse would be poor consolation, but it was better than third.

They rolled into town like a storm off the coast and crossed the line a nose before the other team.

He glanced over, ready to give Briscoe a scathing look, and saw the cold, bitter face of Grim Halver instead.

"Congratulations," said Halver with a thin smile. He pulled his gloves off and trudged up to his leader.

The world went a little strange and distant to Heft as the town swamped him, their awe overcome by excitement this once, shouting themselves hoarse in their excitement, waving their papers, thumping him on the shoulders.

He shouldered through them and went up to his own leader, bending down to rub his head and praise him.

"Mister Heft, may I congratulate you." Stone stumped up to him, pounding his back heartily.

"Thank you." He pulled off his gloves and walked back up the line to throw them in the sled bag. "I didn't think the dogs had it."

"Here is your cut."

"Already?"

Stone only smiled with ineffable pleasure.

Silently, Heft pocketed the money.

"How did he lose?" The question was for Stone, but his eye was on the pale man across the street who was rubbing his dogs one by one. He'd never seen a team look so licked as Halver's.

Stone shrugged. "I suppose your team was just a little better."

"Hmm." Not the right answer. "Whatever gave him the idea to take the shortcut? I saw him come out there. Risky."

"Well, Briscoe did it."

"But Briscoe is a young hothead."

Stone scratched the side of his head thoughtfully. "He's not so much of a hothead anymore. He gets a little older every year, you know…."

"Forget Reuben, I'm not talking about him. Why did Halver take that shortcut?"

"Must have gotten around town that it was a faster route. Also, that *you* never take it."

"For good reason. Did he know about the *bisgak* wintering there?"

"Hum. It's not my fault his dogs like to chase *bisgak*."

"Stone…."

Heft turned to the boys holding his dogs and gave them a nod toward the dog lot. He stalked into the alley beside the outfitters, Stone trailing.

"You set that up, didn't you? Do his dogs run at *bisgak*? Did you know that?"

"How could I?"

There was a flat silence. Heft reached into his coat pocket and shoved the deerhide purse and the folded money at Stone. "It's not fair. Take it back."

"What's unfair about it?"

"You set this race up to make money!"

"That's what a match race is."

"Not the money part, the set up part. You promised me that you would not cheat."

"How did I cheat?" The innocent look was back, more plaintive than ever.

"You told him to take the shortcut, didn't you? Didn't you!" His voice practically shook the worn boards of the outfitters wall.

"No I didn't, I'll even swear I didn't. He just couldn't resist a bet that he'd beat you by a quarter of the course, and hence, he took the shortcut."

"You had that all figured out?"

"My dear Heft, when you've in this business long

enough, you get to be a pretty good judge of men. I may have given him a rope, but he's the one who tied himself in knots. He's only got himself to blame."

Heft muttered under his breath, but the fight eased out of his shoulders and he glanced down at the money.

"What are you going to do with your share?" asked Stone.

"Get as far away from you as I can."

"Now, now, you don't mean that!"

"Try me." He started for the dog lot.

"Anyway, it wouldn't be fair, as I am the one who got you all that money." Stone planted his feet. "And you can't go out of business with me without breaking your word."

"You seem to get me into much more business than I ever agreed to."

"And look where it has got you!"

"Promise me you'll not do this again."

Stone's face went saintly. "Never."

"Shake." Heft held out his hand, and his frosty eye held Stone's gaze hard.

Stone reached out and shook it. Heft released his hand with a sigh.

"I did have one idea...."

"No!" He started quickly across the hard-packed snow.

"Why, Mister Heft!" Stone started after him as fast as his short legs could manage, his hands outstretched in appeal. "It's only business!"

THE MAN WHO LAUGHED IN DEATH'S FACE

7

THE MAN WHO LAUGHED IN DEATH'S FACE

In the Blue Slate range, there is no forgiveness. The peaks rise like the jagged teeth of a wolf's jawbone, covered year-round in sheets of ice and snow ready to fall at any sound. Between the snow and the rockslides, the land changes continually.

Only one pass was ever mapped, named for James Yarnat who mapped it one year and died in it the next.

The men who knew nothing of land, only of papers and orders, set forth a prize for anyone who could find a way back through it, because beyond this impregnable range lay vast, untouched land: high plains and golden hills and purple mountains with good timber.

They called it the Wentworth Prize, and there was a reason no man had done it in the seventy years the challenge had stood.

"Only a bit further, Mister Wood."

Captain Innes lifted his head to the sky as if he could

sense the height of our climb by the air alone. Who am I to judge—maybe he could.

Ahead of us toiled the army scout, Trulove, a fellow who mostly had experience in desert and mountain pathfinding but seemed competent in the face of any terrain.

We'd been climbing the hills for days, beating brush, wading through grasses tall enough to lose yourself in, following the winding river we'd come up. The captain and I carried the wood on our backs, leaving Trulove free to scout out the fastest trail to the ridge. Not that there was much to see at the moment in a sea of towering pines.

We had been pushing, pushing hard, ever since our boats had wrecked about seventy miles upriver. Trulove had even scouted in the dark.

Beyond us, Trulove broke through the trees and lifted his glasses to the west.

"Captain!"

I didn't need to know much to understand his tone. The captain broke into a run and I after him, and we mounted the ridge a moment later, my breath coming hard and the wind in my ears.

Stretched below us was the rocky coast and the sea beyond that, the sun spreading a lapful of gold across its shining expanse. A pair of white specks on the edge of the horizon heralded our death sentence, clear as day.

"Sir—" Trulove looked over at the captain, his dependable face as blank as the blue sky above. "Would you like me to set the fire?"

"No, we both know it won't do any good." He let his load slip off his shoulder to the brown grass.

Days of traveling, and we were three hours too late.

I looked to the captain—I suppose it is an army man's instinct to look to his officer when trouble arises—and his stony face was grim. Worse, there was a jagged emptiness in it.

But then he noticed my gaze, and the look was gone like smoke.

"Private Wood, leave the firewood. We will no longer be needing it."

"Yes, sir."

I swung the load off my shoulder and undid the straps. The wood I had scavenged, that we had carried, that had slowed us—for nothing. I undid the captain's load too, pulled the straps free.

"Your orders, sir?" Trulove squinted into the sun, it was impossible to tell his thoughts through that expression.

"We'll go back to camp."

I cleared my throat.

"What are we going to do, sir? Let them go?" I had to ask. With those sails disappearing over the horizon and our lives and homes disappearing with them, I had a right to ask.

"They would not see us, not if we set the whole coast ablaze. No, private, we go back to the others."

The others, the eighteen men we had left at a base camp—some were injured—were all members of the company that had gone upriver to do some light scouting while the ships refitted.

We three had gone to catch the ships before they sailed, probably believing us dead. Now we were as good as.

"Did you hear me, Private Wood?"

"Yes, sir. Back to camp."

I saluted, but even that felt wrong up there on that desolate rocky hill with the wind blowing and blowing.

EVEN AFTER A WEEK, with over a dozen men to salvage and set up a camp, the beach was littered with wreckage. The remains of the three expedition boats, the provisions, everything that could be salvaged sat to one side, dragged up between the river and the trees. On the sandy spit, the extra canvases had been stretched over poles cut from pine branches, making makeshift shelters.

Two horses, the officers' mounts, were tied to one side. They had been lame when we left; otherwise we would have taken them and surely caught the ships in time.

The first man who spotted us was Lieutenant Sanborn, a fresh-faced blond fellow, tall as a tree and almost too young to be a lieutenant. Being an officer, he'd had some training and could perform the basic duties of a doctor. At the moment, he was knee-deep in the shallows of the river, washing bandages.

"Captain!" Ever dutiful, Sanborn set down the bandages and shoved his arms into his green jacket, buttoning it hastily. I could see it on his face—the hope that his military efficiency could not hide.

Captain Innes motioned briefly for him to follow and they went down the shore a little ways, alone.

The men trickled out to us like smoke from the barrel of a discharged cannon.

"Well?" The men faced us, Trulove and I, their faces worried.

"The captain will tell you, I am sure," said Trulove (that

man could stay nonchalant facing a catamount) and went down to the river to refill his canteen.

I followed him because I didn't know what else to do with their eyes staring at me, all losing hope. Good news doesn't need to keep; it's the bad news that waits.

"I sure'd hate to be the one to tell them." I crouched on the pebbly shore beside him, glancing back at the men who were talking amongst themselves now.

"If anyone can do it, it's the captain," said Trulove. "Ah, here comes Sergeant Nolan."

Nolan sauntered up. Unlike Sanborn with his careful polish, the sergeant had discarded his jacket, his shirt unbuttoned halfway and his sleeves rolled to the elbows. His head was gray, but his charmer's face was young yet, as if his hair had prematurely turned.

"They left, didn't they?" His voice was low enough that the men couldn't catch it.

"Yep." Trulove did not hesitate. "They left."

Nolan turned his head away as a man might turn away to spit, and he swore softly.

"What's the captain think?" he asked, once he had gotten that off his chest.

"He's kept his own counsel since three days ago when we missed them. He's talking with Sanborn now." Trulove nodded toward the two men walking further down the shore.

"And without a doubt, we missed them?"

"Saw the sails disappear over the horizon myself."

"Hm." Nolan folded his arms and lifted his chin to the tumbling river. "That hardly bodes well for us, does it?"

Trulove replaced the top of his canteen slowly. "Well, I

don't know what the captain intends, but I have a wife and two little girls back home. I ain't giving up that easy."

He threw the canteen over one shoulder and started back across the sand to the meager pile of salvaged supplies.

Jeremiah, our cartographer, was leaned up against one of the crates, his left arm cradled to his chest in a sling, the other hand scribbling away at the sketchbook that lay on his leg.

"You have the worst luck, son—I need into that crate."

Without a word, Jeremiah lifted his pen, moved forward an arm's length, and resumed where he had left off.

Trulove pried the lid off the crate and began to rummage through it.

"How many of your surveying instruments do you still have, Jeremiah?" he asked after a minute or two.

"One of each, no extras. They were washed away. All the paper got wet, but I managed to dry most of it out, so it can be used."

"You may need it."

The captain returned to take stock of the situation, Sanborn trailing behind. Innes nodded to Nolan—the two of them were close, and he seemed to take it for granted that Sergeant Nolan understood the situation. As for Jeremiah, you could probably shoot a cannon over his head and he'd keep working.

"What do we have, Mr. Trulove?"

"One map that's not ruined. Won't be much help—it's land to the southwest of us. Unless we are going to try the coast."

"I don't see any point in that, do you?"

"No, sir, I don't."

"Then it's forward, Mr. Trulove. Straight into those high plains."

Trulove touched his forehead. "Yes, sir."

The Captain turned his gaze to the rest of us. "I am going to address the men. If you have objections, I would like you to voice them now, not after."

Not one of us stirred.

"Lawson, how are you?" Captain Innes took a step closer to Jeremiah.

Jeremiah glanced up. It took someone like the captain to break his concentration when he was working.

"Just fine, sir." He saluted with his pen in his fingers.

"That arm going to bother you?"

"I can travel fine, map just as well. Might be a little slower with my instruments."

"Good."

Captain Innes passed him by and crossed the spit of sand to the rest of the men, who had been milling around, watching us with growing concern.

"I know you are all wondering it, so I may as well speak plainly because there's no gentle way of putting it. The ships left us behind."

If the men had begun to complain, I would have understood. But the silence—the silence struck the fear of death into my own heart.

"However, we are not dead yet and I do not intend for us to be. We will march east, toward those mountains. There is plenty of water and game, so provisions will not be a problem."

"What about when we get to the mountains?" one of the men asked. Jackson was his name, a fellow with heavy eyes and a thick mustache.

"We'll go through Yarnat Pass if need be. And we'll not just bring two men through alive, we'll bring twenty."

"All due respect, sir, no one gets through Yarnat pass."

"It's been done, if you recall." Innes said the thing as if it was child's play and turned to address Trulove.

"Not in seventy bloody years," Jackson persisted. "That's suicide."

"Men," —Innes swung around on his heel— "we are not dying."

Another voice weighed in on Jackson's side. "Sir—they say Yarnat Pass is impassable now."

"It's death of exposure or falling from a cliff," added another, emboldened.

"Is that so?"

I didn't like the expression that was coming over Innes's face.

He looked down, drew his pistol and cocked it, refusing to look at them, his face as cold and hard as the iron in his hands.

"All right, then. Any cowards can step out now, and I'll put them out of their misery."

He dragged his hard gaze over the men in front of him, and then, for good measure, raked it over the rest of us standing by his side. I hadn't any intention of buckling under the prospect of Yarnat Pass, and he knew it, but it felt like crawling over glass, those few seconds his eyes were on me.

Then a smile broke over his face like summer sunshine and he laughed, thrusting his pistol back in his belt. "Well then, I'm glad to see I have the best men on God's green earth at my side. Let's get moving!"

. . .

We followed the river for the first few days, resting for the injured and taking the route that was easiest on the horses, who were still slow and sore. But when the river bent back to the northwest, we parted company with it and set a course due east towards the distant mountains.

We had paused for a rest one afternoon. I was sharing a canteen with Wade, a grim-faced fellow and a crack shot, one of the best I'd ever seen. Not far from us, Sanborn knelt beside Jeremiah, checking the bandage on the splint.

Wade looked over, rubbing his beard in hesitant curiosity. "How's the arm?"

"Well, I'm no Joseph Drucker," said Sanborn, keeping his eyes on the bandage as he wound it. "But he'll use it again."

"It's good it was my left arm that broke." Jeremiah spoke with a degree of measured cheer. "It does not slow my work much."

"I'm still assigning you an assistant." Sanborn tore the bandage in his teeth and tied it off. "Take your pick. Whoever you want, you've got him."

The mapmaker's eyes lit on me. "Wood will do." Then to me, "It won't be hard."

Hard wasn't what I was worried about—tedious was more like it—but I smiled to reassure him I didn't mind.

From that day on I followed him, held his inks and papers, and helped him take readings, all the way across the wide, golden plains.

. . .

"The grass is turning." Jeremiah thrust his pen in his teeth and reached down to pluck a couple seed heads off a stalk of grass. "Means we don't have long before winter."

He straightened and regarded the horizon shrewdly. With plentiful game and Trulove scouting on horseback now, we had traveled quickly and eaten well; but we were under the shadow of the mountains now. Before long, we'd be counting our progress by feet, not miles, with freezing faces and bleeding feet. Our boots were already worn from the march, and I did not want to imagine how they would be after a few days in the mountains.

Trulove came back at an easy canter, drawing swift rein right beside us. The wind blew his black hair wrong way round; the scent of it was crisp, promising cold.

"Jeremiah." Trulove touched his forehead in greeting, though Jeremiah was not his senior.

Jeremiah returned it briefly. "Trulove, how far do you figure?"

"Fifteen miles, perhaps, to the mountains themselves. Another day before we start really ascending."

"I figured it was about that."

"Yeah. But good ground before then. We'll have it easy enough up until the last."

Jeremiah gave a brief chuckle.

"We'll take what we can get, right?" Wade came up and set down his share of the supply load, shaking back his hair. He hadn't cut it for weeks—Sanborn was far less a barber than a doctor, and some of the men preferred to forgo the risks. I had suffered his butchery, as I hated hair tickling my ears, but the next time I looked in a pool of water, I wasn't sure I ever wanted to see myself again.

"It's all we have," muttered Trulove. Then aloud, "Seen Nolan?"

"Back a ways." Wade shoved a thumb over his shoulder.

"Good." Trulove turned his horse, and it tossed its head and lifted off the ground in protest. He drew rein and backed it next to Jeremiah. "I'm only saying this because I think you've already figured it. We're going to have to take Yarnat. There's nothing out there."

"Yeah, figured so." Jeremiah was as calm about his figuring as a man would be sitting in front of his own fire.

"It won't be enjoyable, breaking it to the captain and officers. Anyhow, thought we could use some good eating before we try it—" Trulove reached around his saddle horn and unwrapped a short rope, tossing down a fat string of dead fowl.

"Got us some prairie hen."

THE NIGHT WAS SOMBER.

One of the boys was playing a mouth harp, some sweet, sad tune about sweethearts with sunshine in their gleaming hair. In the orange firelight, Jeremiah was still working, but he considered me off duty now. Anything he did after supper, he took on his own bony shoulders.

"Do you know what they're saying about us back home, boys?" Innes leaned on his arms, his eyes gleaming dark in the firelight.

The music stopped.

No one answered, waiting for what he would say, but Lieutenant Sanborn leaned forward, his arms on his knees.

"They're saying, 'This is it. This is the expedition, the accident that finally does old Captain Innes in.'"

A brief chuckle went around, mostly bravado.

"And they'd be right. They should be right. But they won't be. Because it's us they speak of. Sanborn, Nolan, Trulove, every man of you. Any other group of men, I'd have pronounced us dead in a week. But with you men, we'll walk right up to their doorsteps, or crawl if we have to, and say to them: 'You gave us up for dead. But you forgot who you were dealing with. I'm a man of Roger Innes's company and we laugh in death's face!'"

Sanborn and Wade were grinning. Lean, grim smiles. Nolan was nodding. But Trulove only studied the gun he was cleaning, his cloth over one knee, his thick brows knit.

The captain's eye came to rest on him. "Trulove, I know you have something to say—come, spit it out. From this moment on, we keep nothing from each other."

"It's the scouting, sir. I'm not sure the horses are suited to the pass, and it'll be a sight slower without them."

"We'll take them. If we have to shoot and eat them halfway, so be it."

This did not seem to reassure Trulove. He made no effort to speak further, but I felt a distinct discomfort.

If Trulove was uneasy, he knew something we didn't. And despite Innes's urging that we keep nothing from each other, Trulove still felt it was better left unsaid. That alone made me afraid, deep in my middle, against the inside of my spine.

But the mood around the fire had lightened with the captain's words.

"Do you have a song, sir?" asked the man with the mouth harp, hopefully, his trusty instrument out again.

Innes frowned, thinking. "Well, you know I haven't much of a voice."

"You don't have to sing if you don't wish to, sir."

"Do you know, 'We're Going Home At Last'?"

"Know it like my own fireside."

The man started the song, plaintively, with the mouth harp, but the men joined in, lusty and loud. It was a soldier's song, the sort one sings after a campaign when he's half mad to be home with good cooking and soft beds and trying not to remember how many comrades will never again share those joys. The sort one sings when he's trying not to remember it might be his turn next.

We sang and sang against the night, trying to hold tomorrow at bay.

THE MEN HAD, at last, laid down to sleep. The watch had been set, and I was off on a voluntary errand for Jeremiah, drawing fresh water from the stream a hundred yards outside the camp so he could make another batch of makeshift ink.

It was on my way back that the captain's voice, near at hand, stopped me.

"I told them we would have no secrets, and I meant it. But you men—I must speak with you plain."

I paused, unseen and unwilling to break in. Innes stood outside the circle by the fire. With him, by the orange cast of light, I could see Sanborn, straight as a ramrod; Nolan, smoking as he does of nights; Trulove, with his dark eyebrows knit.

"I trust you men with my life," the captain went on quietly. "If something happens to me, I want your word that you'll pull the others through. No quitting."

Sanborn folded his arms slowly. "I'd march them over the mouth of hell if you gave the word."

"And you know I'm not about to die and let those stuffed shirts back home think you failed," Nolan guffawed, spewing a stream of smoke as if it were right in those desk-officer's faces.

"Trulove?"

Trulove stirred, clearing his throat. "Of course, sir. I don't think you need my affidavit to know I'm in this to the hilt."

Captain Innes smiled, the iron lines in his face gentling. "No, Trulove, of course not." He reached out and slapped the man on the shoulder.

"Then I have your word? Because this pass is going to be like nothing we've faced before. We're hardly dressed for it, our shoes are going to fall apart, and we'll likely begin to starve. It's going to be as ugly as war. And we won't have an enemy to unite against—just ourselves."

"Lead on, Captain." Sanborn gave a nod toward the pass, cloaked in the darkness. "We're behind you."

Captain Innes reached out to clasp the men's hands, and it seemed to me almost as if they knew they were saying goodbye.

I left then. It was not something I should be witnessing.

When exactly we left the hills and entered the mountain, no one was sure—the land just got colder and rockier and meaner until we came upon a pile of rocks, stacked in a way that only could be man-made.

"Take a look at this." Trulove knocked the dust and snow off a broad, flat rock beside the formation.

Mouth of Yarnat Pass, James Yarnat did build this memorial for Roger Catsby who did perish in the pass, one day before the end. Thomas Preston.

"Quite a man, was Preston. Didn't go back with Yarnat the next year. Drank away his regrets," Innes said softly.

He bent down to examine the roughly carved words for himself and then straightened, glancing around at the men. "Well, lads, this is it! Right over those mountains is home!"

The cheers were loud, louder than I had expected. Enough to make Jeremiah look up from his careful study of the slanting mountains before us. "What is it?"

"This is the mouth of the pass," I said. "He told the men home is just over those mountains."

Jeremiah frowned gently. "Well, it's a sight more complicated than that."

"You should keep that yourself, then." I shouldered his bag with a little smile. "The men are counting on it."

He looked at me strangely, then smiled back. "I guess you're right."

I shifted my feet and leaned closer to him. I caught the heavy smell of unwashed hair and the sharp tang of ink. "What do you think our chances are?"

"You probably don't want to know what I think. Besides, I'm only the mapmaker."

"Besides the captain and Trulove, I think you know the most about what lies ahead of us."

He sighed, looking at me and then at the dirt-drifted path in front of us. "We'd be lucky to make it out. And I don't think all of us will."

I didn't answer him right away.

"But it might be me whose time is up." He gives me a

smile, as if that's somehow supposed to comfort me. "You never know."

"I suppose it doesn't do to try to predict any of it," I answered wryly. "Tell me, what are we doing next?"

WE HAD BEEN in the pass a week when it happened. We were hungry but not yet starved, our boots worn through, our hands bloodied with climbing, our faces frozen. Every night our store of bandages and whiskey wore thinner as we patched ourselves up. The length between us and the rolling plains behind grew ever greater, but the distance ahead seemed to remain the same.

Trulove was ahead, scouting, with a couple men helping to clear the path where it was the most blocked or buried. It was slow work, but we were moving forward.

The ground suddenly gave a shiver and then a long, low tremor. Low thunder became a terrific roar and there was a long scream, cut off.

"The scouts!" uttered Sanborn and Nolan as one.

They broke into a run.

I stayed with Jeremiah, who was still taking a reading and had barely noticed the commotion, but a feeling of dread settled in my stomach. A rockslide could sweep away the men up ahead, and we'd never find them.

And Trulove was our only scout.

"What is it?" Innes came striding up from the rear where he had been helping along the stragglers. We had more and more men dropping behind as each day passed.

"Rockslide, I think." My voice was thick in the cold air.

"Up ahead?"

I nodded, and he reached up and touched his nose as if he wanted to put his entire head in his hands.

"Go up there, tell me the short of it. Run."

I saluted and ran.

It was a rockslide. Shale and broken rock and settling dust mingled. I came up just in time to see Sanborn draw his pistol, muffling it with the sleeve of his coat, and shoot downwards.

It must have been the horse.

The report echoed, but nothing more fell.

He pulled his coat back on, smoking hole and all.

Jackson was shaking rock dust out of his hair with a few colorful oaths, and Nolan was helping him up.

"Captain wants a report," I said, finding my voice at last.

Sanborn didn't seem to hear me. He was kneeling down just then, and Nolan started towards me. I met him partway and saw that it was Trulove on the ground, one leg twisted entirely the wrong way. Trulove was not a weak man; though he was pale and soaked in sweat, he didn't make a sound.

"Jackson's all right." Nolan jerked his gray head in the man's direction. "Horse is dead, Hobbs is dead. Trulove—"

Trulove's voice broke in, quiet but steady. "Sanborn, just tell the captain. I can't go on, you know that."

"Aw, don't talk that way." Sanborn glanced up and motioned for Nolan to rip up something for bandages. "You're going home to see those little girls of yours. Think how much they'll have grown. You'll want to see that."

"You know there's no way I can travel or you can get out hauling me."

"You leave that to us." Sanborn's gaze whipped

between the three of us and picked me out. "Go tell the captain, get him up here as quick as you can."

Innes was waiting for me at the bend, a deep scowl on his face. It disappeared the moment he saw me.

"Hobbs is dead, Trulove's injured bad. Jackson's all right. Sanborn had to shoot the horse."

"I figured when I heard the shot. Sanborn or Nolan say anything?"

"Sanborn sent me to get you, wants you as quick as you can come."

"Show me the way."

By the time we made it back, the horrendous angle of Trulove's leg was corrected and he was white as wool, Sanborn fashioning a splint out of a couple rifle ramrods.

There was no wood out here save scrubby bushes.

Innes crouched down beside them.

"Sorry, Captain," Trulove murmured. "Came out of nowhere. Nothing we could have done."

"I know."

"And Hobbs, I—"

"Not your fault." Innes's voice was actually gentle. I had never heard it like that before.

"I tried to tell Sanborn it won't do no good. This leg is busted."

Innes shook his head. "We are not leaving you. You have brought us this far—we will be through before long, and you must get the credit for what you have done. You'll come if I have to carry you over my own shoulders."

Trulove gave a faint smile, and in that moment, his acquiescence seemed an even braver thing than his offer to stay behind. We couldn't wait, and in any other situation, he shouldn't move. I didn't envy him the rest of the journey.

Innes straightened and shrugged off his coat.

"Get another coat, rig a stretcher. If you need to trade off coats to stay warm, then so be it."

Nolan and Sanborn both started to remove their coats. Nolan threw his down.

He cleared his throat and lowered his voice. "Captain, who is going to scout?"

"I will," he said quietly. "I'm not risking anyone else up the trail."

"But Cap—Roger, we need you to lead us."

A small smile lit Innes's face, and he slapped his friend's arm. "That, my good fellow, is precisely what I intend to do."

I STOOD up from beside the coals and swung my frozen arms to get the blood moving back through them, looking up at the gray-blue of the slate wall towering above us. It was shrouded in mist and cloud so that you couldn't see the top of it. The air was thin and so cold that I didn't know how I'd convince my feet to keep going.

A faint ripple went through the company as Innes materialized through the mist, coming back up the trail.

"All right, men." His voice was low, as faint as the wisp of half-hearted smoke that rose from our sad fire. "We have to move out now. We keep moving or we freeze. And we keep the silence in the ranks again today."

We had walked in the shadow of heavy snows the last three days, the threat of avalanche quite literally over our heads. No one was allowed to raise their voices over a whisper, and the men, hungry and cold, were looking more and more dispirited. Since Jeremiah rarely talked anyway, there wasn't much change for me.

The men got to their feet, but I had seen cattle more willing. Something was going to break.

It came that afternoon, as the day was beginning to wane, the sun falling behind us. Innes had brought us to a narrow strip, barely a horse's width, with a wall of slate on one side and on the other a sheer drop to jagged rocks a few hundred feet down.

We were forced to let the last horse go, for it was nervous and would not suffer itself to be blindfolded. That was what started to unsettle the men, I think. It felt like an unraveling of control, even if it were a measured calculation.

After another half mile, we stopped to give Trulove a rest. The man was a soldier to the bone and never complained, but Jackson seemed to feel a responsibility for having emerged from the accident almost unscathed, and Sanborn had taken it upon himself to oversee things personally. They asked for rests, and Innes did not refuse.

No one liked crouching along the narrow rock, the snow towering above our heads. Our faces were frozen, our shirts stuck to our chests with sweat underneath our coats. We were going to be chilled through before long.

"How long is the strip?" asked Jeremiah softly, all business. He had his notebook gripped in his left fingers, his pen poised to take note. His arm was considerably better—I only continued to assist him because it helped keep my mind off our plight.

"Five, six miles, the captain said. Maybe a little more."

There was a stir among the men.

"Quiet, keep your voices down," ordered Innes, soft but sharp.

"You can't expect us to risk our necks like that," protested one man, getting to his feet. "There has to be another way."

"There isn't one. I would have taken you another way if there was."

"Well, I ain't dying for this. If we hurry, we can back-track. It's easier going down than up."

"We have a descent ahead of us," said Sanborn. He had gone tense like a dog on the edge of a fight, but Innes stood as calmly as if he was in his own house.

One of the men drew his pistol and brandished it. "You have to let us go."

"Don't be fools." Innes's voice was low, his breath standing almost still on the thin, frozen air. "You shoot, we'll all be buried."

"You shout, we'll be buried," added Sanborn, in a husky voice that was going thin.

"Then you had better not stop us."

There were six or seven of them now, nodding, gathering. Jeremiah and I were behind them, the captain and the officers in front of them. They could turn and bolt, just like that.

Innes's voice stayed calm, but he raised it just a hair. "I'm going to tell you again, and only once. You don't want to do this."

Jeremiah glanced up as if realizing our situation for the first time. He handed me his pen and closed his notebook, slowly.

He handed that to me too.

The men were in heated discussion with Innes, and no one saw Jeremiah coming up the path, planting himself in the middle of a narrow spit, barely enough for his two feet.

If he felt the threat of the wild emptiness below him, it didn't show.

"You cannot force us, Captain. We are leaving."

They turned and found themselves face to face with Jeremiah.

"Don't stop us."

I saw the strange, mad fear in their eyes.

"Lawson…." There was warning in the captain's tone. I am not sure if he was warning Jeremiah against letting them through or trying to warn him how mad they had gone.

"Let us through, Jeremiah." The first man took a step toward him, his hand on his gun.

"No." His voice barely carried to me, standing just behind him.

Any other man, it would have been just a word. From Jeremiah, it was a thunderclap.

A thunderclap that cracked and then crumbled their brittle resolve. I could not see his face, only the iron set to his too-thin shoulders, but that was enough.

The gumption went out of the men with a tired, tired sigh.

"Men, you are weary and cold and you have gone through more in these last weeks than most men do in an entire campaign. There is nothing more to be said, by me or anyone else." Innes's glance went to Sanborn, who nodded. "Let's move out."

Jeremiah took the notebook and pen back as if nothing

had happened. The streak of iron that had held back a mad tide was gone, and I never saw it again.

THE NEXT MORNING, Sergeant Nolan got out his razor and shaved his face clean as a child's. Frost thick as ice lay over everything; it was so cold and the air so thin that we had slept in groups to keep each other warm.

But we were in a sheltered place where there was no danger of an avalanche, and the narrow paths were gone. We were back on wide ground, rocky and slippery though it was.

Nolan hummed happily to himself as he felt along his face and slid the razor after it, no cream, no mirror.

"What's the idea?" asked Jackson, amused. He wouldn't shave, even given the chance—his heavy mustache now had a beard to go with it.

"Have to look the part of an officer," Nolan said cheerily.

A low murmur passed among the men. Fifteen sets of eyes were on him now.

Nolan produced a short stub of a cigarette and lit it. "Last one." He smiled roguishly around it. "Been saving it, but now there's no need."

"No need?" Wade gave a half smile and a laugh, as he does when he doesn't quite understand.

"We'll be through this pass and out to Archer's Point by the end of the week. And I'll get a standard issue off the first man I see, if I have to beg or steal it."

Jackson folded his arms. "We're that close?"

"Jeremiah figures it so."

All eyes went to the Captain and Jeremiah talking across

the fire. Physically, the captain was a gaunt shadow of his former self, but the fire in his eyes was unmistakable.

"You mean it?" Wade raised his eyebrows.

"Sure I do." Nolan took the stub out of his mouth and gave a long, contented sigh.

Innes got up. His legs shook a little under him, but the only one who seemed to notice was Nolan. Something I did not understand crossed his face as he looked the captain's way.

Sanborn got up slowly, taking his cue from the captain, and went over to Trulove, who was sitting up drinking coffee. Trulove, too, was only a shadow of himself; but he was alive, and that was more than some had thought possible.

"Let's move out, men." Innes took a few stiff steps over to the men and stood ramrod straight, trying not to sway with weariness. "We have been long on this journey that no man believed we could make. We aren't doing it for the prize or for the glory. We're doing it for the wives and the children and the mothers we left behind." His voice gave briefly. We were all short of breath up here. "We're doing it for them."

As one, the men got up, their resolve renewed.

I didn't know until later, much later, that Nolan had been bluffing. He didn't know any more than the rest of us how much further we had to go.

THE OUTPOST of Archer's Point was the last bastion of civilization before the Blue Slate mountains. It was never manned by more than fifteen men—a backwater job for people who go nowhere.

The dawn watch was just coming on duty when we stumbled from the mist, twenty wasted men, little more than skin and bones.

We marched right up to the gates, or rather, limped and dragged, some men half-carrying the man beside them. There was Jeremiah, his shirt hanging off his bony shoulders, his fingers stained with ink, a full and better mapping of the Yarnat pass in his bag; Sanborn and Wade, barely able to keep their own heads up, carrying Trulove between them; Nolan's haggard face lifted proudly despite a heavy limp.

And at our heads, a weary, swaying figure, dark beard clinging where it could to his skeletal face, his once-white shirt torn in a dozen places, a handkerchief tying up the worst of his cuts.

"Who goes?" called the lieutenant from the open gates, his voice uncertain, like he was facing the supernatural, not men.

Innes took a steady step towards him, saluting.

"Captain Roger Innes, reporting twenty-one souls alive, one—"

He pitched forward and they caught him as he fell.

In the Blue Slate range, there is no forgiveness. The peaks rise like the jagged teeth of a wolf's jawbone, covered year-round in sheets of ice and snow ready to fall at any sound. Between the snow and the rockslides, the land changes continually.

The men who finally conquered it made history. Captain Roger Innes, who held his men together by sheer courage; the young mapmaker, who charted a clear and traceable route; Trulove, the scout whose supplementary routes saved countless lives in the years to come.

They said we had nerve, said we laughed in death's face —the men who won the Wentworth Prize that no man had won in seventy years.

But we didn't set out to win the prize, and that is what made the difference.

We were just going home.

FOLLOW THE WIND

8

FOLLOW THE WIND

The word was out in town: new money.

It started at the outfitters, where the army captain had shown up looking for dog-drivers to push north into the teeth of winter. From there it spread to the Pick and Collarbone, and then to every house and shanty for fifty miles around.

There were nigh on two hundred men preparing to winter nearby, with nothing to do and money to burn.

And what Kaquom had was good dogs. Good dogs for racing.

LARAMIE BENT OVER HIS FIRE, humming a little under his breath as he stirred and poked the flames to life. With a clang, he hung his pot over the range, filled with fresh snow from the night before.

"Morning." Sergeant Nolan was coming by, a thick scarf wound around his neck and covering his mouth and nose. "Mind if I share your fire?"

"Not at all." Laramie dusted the snow off his gloves and turned to get the coffee tin.

"I say, I don't know a single man in this army who keeps his fire so well or has the coffee hot so early. If I was the captain, I'd sure have taken you and not Peck."

Laramie guffawed. "Well, it's a good thing he didn't ask, because I might just have disobeyed orders for the first time in my life. I'm not as young as I once was, and these lean bones sure don't want to die swimming in snow."

Nolan laughed under his scarf, his pale eyes bright. "I'll tell you, I've been everywhere but hell itself with Roger Innes, but I wasn't angry when that lieutenant took my place." He held up his hands. "But don't you breathe a word of that to the captain."

"No sir." Laramie touched his forehead with a couple fingers in salute.

"Fact is, it'll be job enough keeping these men in hand for a winter this long. The locals say it could easily be another five or six months before things thaw out."

Laramie clucked and shook his head. "Don't envy you the job, sir."

"Well, it'll be easier before the weather turns heavy. There's a dog race coming up, the men are raring to bet on it." He fished a cigarette out of his coat pocket and lit it with a twig pulled from the fire. "A waste of money, I think, but they'll be happy."

The cigarette lit with a puff of smoke and he tossed the twig back into the fire.

"A dog race?"

"With those sleds. You know, teams."

"Ah."

"Apparently it's a serious thing around here. A man could get rich if he handled things right."

Laramie only chuckled in reply. "Well, I've got to get the podge finished."

"Right." Nolan got to his feet. "The men'll be by before long, cold and hungry."

"And mean as bears." Laramie's mustache quirked in a half-smile.

Nolan breathed out a stream of smoke and smiled. "Keep that fire hot. I'll be back."

"It'll always be hot for you, Sergeant."

The men materialized from the thinning darkness of the morning, swinging arms and blowing on stiff hands, their voices blending in a low hum of excitement.

"Is it true that there's a dog race comin' up?" asked Laramie, ladling out hot breakfast to the first man in line.

"Sure enough. Though the locals say some of the best teams went north with the captain. So it's anyone's game where the betting's concerned."

"That so?"

"They say the two best dog drivers left in town are one Epirvikk Heft who's a major figure in these parts and don't race. The other one's a man they call Spruce, but word is, he won't race neither."

"So bets are open." The man behind him rubbed his hands eagerly. "I'm going with Aki Dunlap. Those dogs look fit to run a hundred miles."

Laramie just stirred the podge quietly and listened.

The Pick and Collarbone was full to brimming when Laramie wandered in sometime after moonrise. Smoke hung low around the oil lamps, and laughter and the smell of spirits and unwashed men filled the dim room.

Locals and soldiers mingled without restraint, swapping tales and boasts. He'd never seen anything like it down south—there was something about the savage winters here that drew men together instead of driving them apart.

The bartender came over as he stepped up to the counter. "What'll you have?"

"Want to know if you know a man named Spruce. A dog-driver, I hear."

"Over there. You can't miss him." He nodded to a dim corner. "Fellow's a trapper. You call him a dog-driver and he might just walk out on you."

"But he drives dogs?"

"Never seen a better."

"Thanks." Laramie gave the man a nod and turned to head over.

The man the bartender had pointed out was a tall fellow with a thin beard and legs that reached clear to the other end of the scrawny table where he sat. He wore a hat—odd for indoors—pulled low over his brow.

The table in front of him was empty.

"Table looks a little lonesome with nothing on it." Laramie paused casually as if just passing. "Can I buy you a drink?"

Spruce raised his face slowly. His eyes were a pebbled-river blue, taking Laramie in carefully, from the dirty camp coat to the lean, weathered face.

"Sorry, I don't drink, old man."

"Pity. If you were in the army, you'd probably learn."

"I don't put no stock in the army." He leaned back and pulled his hat down over his eyes.

"Well, maybe you don't, and many's the man who's been bettered by steering clear of the uniform, but I sure do put stock in you."

Under the hat, all he could see was a dimple from a smile. "You'd be the first."

"You don't bluff well, son. Word is half this town puts stock in what you can do."

Spruce sat up, threw his hat onto the table and combed back his thick blond hair with his fingers. "Even if they did, I wouldn't do it for them."

"Your food." A small, black-haired woman, barely more than a girl, was standing just behind him, holding a plate of stew and a mug of coffee.

Spruce smiled, just a little, and reached out to take it from her. "Thank you, Hanni."

As he reached up, Laramie saw he was missing two fingers on his left hand, which had been in his coat pocket until now.

"It's the good coffee," Hanni whispered, and turned quickly to leave.

"Would you bring out a mug of it for my friend here?"

She turned back just long enough to give a shy nod.

Laramie sank into a seat. "Folk say you have good dogs. And you know how to handle a team."

"Yep."

"And all those fools talking about racing, they say you'd be the man to beat."

"Maybe, but I'm not going to be racing." He let out a sigh and put his feet up on the chair opposite. "I'm heading up north tomorrow, to run my traps. Same way those fools that left you behind are going."

"'Fools' may be my personal opinion too, in this

weather, but I don't recollect hearing Captain Innes called a fool before."

"Innes, huh?" A spark of interest lit in his eyes.

"You know him?"

"No." The answer came solid and a little too fast. It wasn't a lie, but it wasn't quite everything.

Hanni returned with the second coffee, and Spruce dug a coin out of his pocket for her.

"Keep the rest," he said quietly.

Laramie sipped the coffee slowly. "So you're going north, alone in this weather?"

"I've been through worse." Spruce took a generous bite of his stew.

"Why not stay the winter here?"

"Had to come south because I lost five good dogs to a bull *tuttik*. And that was the only reason. All my trap lines are north."

"A *tuttik* took down five of your dogs?"

Spruce gave him a slow stare. "Nearly killed me too, except I was carrying a friend's shotgun at the time. Three barrels, it took."

"Lucky, then."

Spruce shrugged. "Well, I'm in debt to Mr. Heft over there." He gave a nod in the direction of a grim-faced fellow with an eyepatch who was leaning against the bar. "Five dogs are expensive, whichever way you put it."

"By how much?"

Spruce's lip curled and he busied himself scraping off his plate.

"Fine. The sum don't matter, because you go into partnership with me, and just one race would fix that."

The tall trapper gave the faintest of smiles. "So that's what you're after."

"There's a reason for the old saying that you don't bet against the man who cooks for the camp. He hears more in one mess hour than a foot soldier hears in his lifetime."

Spruce dragged his legs off the chair with a thump and began to unfold his length from behind the table. "Well, you're out of luck. I don't bet either."

"You don't need to bet. You just run, and I'll give you a cut of the winnings."

Spruce picked his hat up off the table and shoved it onto his head. "Sorry. Like I said, I'm leaving in the morning."

He strode away, leaving Laramie at the table with his half-finished coffee and the empty dishes.

A crash sounded beside the bar.

Laramie craned his neck to see a rough customer gripping the girl by her arm, pressing her back against the bar. A bottle and a couple glasses were smashed, and by the sharp smell filling the air, it was good brandy spreading across the floor.

"You *tuttik* cow," the man snarled. "Watch where you're going!"

Heft, at the bar, raised himself off his elbow, his one good eye watching the situation like a cat, but it was Spruce who was there first.

"Do you want to unhand the lady?"

His voice was slow, almost lazy, the way a snake goes still the moment before it strikes.

"That's a whole bottle of—" He shook the girl as he spoke, and he never finished.

Spruce's fist laid him out in the middle of the glass and brandy.

"Now are you going to apologize and pay for that, or do you want another?" Spruce took a step, towering over the man.

"Now, Spruce!" men were calling. "Leave be! It's just a girl, nothing to start a fight over!" Spruce looked up, taking stock of the speakers, as if they were next.

Laramie had seen enough fights to recognize the smell in the air. This place was as taut as a fiddle string. He abandoned his coffee and headed the nearest way to the door.

It was snowing outside. Bitter cold too, but a relief compared to the stinging air inside the Pick and Collarbone. And it was quiet. Somewhere far off in the dog lots a team was howling, but nothing else broke the stillness of the falling snow.

Laramie shoved his hands in his pockets and trudged down the street towards the camp. Pity about Spruce. The man was as set as a mule.

"Hey, you! Old man!"

Laramie halted and looked around at the empty, snow-covered street.

Spruce came running up on his long legs, panting a little. A trickle of blood ran down his jaw and into his collar.

"Did you mean what you said, that you could get enough in one race for a decent cut?"

"More than decent."

"I'll do it." He held out his hand and then stopped. "I don't know your name."

"Laramie. Yours?"

"You know it."

"You have to have some other name, boy."

"Since when does a man have to have more than one name?"

"Spruce ain't your real name, I know that. I can't do business with a man who don't give me at least one real name."

"Spruce Norman, then," he said, reluctantly. "But no one calls me that."

"Good enough for me. Shake?"

Spruce held out his hand and they sealed it.

"Now, how about another cup of coffee and we can talk? I'll give you something for your face?"

"No thanks. I told you I don't put much stock in armies, and I meant it."

"No one will be there who you haven't seen at the Pick and Collarbone. Besides, my fire's pretty lonely this time of night."

Spruce hesitated.

"Come on. I'll treat you to my best."

It was dark, but in the moonlight it seemed that he flushed.

"It's that little nip that makes the difference." Laramie leaned over and splashed some whiskey into Spruce's tin cup. "On the long marching days, guess who lasts longer on the march, the men from around my fire or the ones from the company over? Mine. It's that splash of whiskey in the coffee, all it takes to get that edge on the next man."

Spruce was tilting the tin coffee cup skeptically.

"And you're saying I'll win if I just find that whisker of advantage?" His eyes flicked up to Laramie's. "I've seen my share of things, my friend. But it's not that simple."

"You are the splash of whiskey. I have no need for other advantages," said Laramie, corking the yellowed-label bottle.

"An awful lot of stock you put in hearsay." Spruce glanced up. "What if I'm no good?"

A smile moved the corner of Laramie's long mustache. "You're good."

"You speak mighty big for a man who doesn't know this country."

"I don't need to know the country—I only need to know men. And I can read a man like a book."

Spruce laughed under his breath and tasted the coffee gingerly. "It's not bad," he admitted.

"Thirty years can't be wrong." Laramie stirred the fire industriously.

"Hm."

"So your trap lines are up north. What makes it different from trap lines down here?"

"I have a stake outside of Chegak." Spruce took another sip and cradled the tin mug in his long hands.

"Is it better up there?"

"It's further north."

Laramie said nothing to that. He studied Spruce's face in the firelight.

"Something wrong?" Spruce glanced up from his cup.

"No. But you have the look of a man who's running from something."

"I'd leave now, but you'd take that to mean you're right." Spruce's voice held a touch of ice.

"Am I wrong, then?"

"Look here. The natives have this word, *ranitaak.* Means follower-of-the-wind. Doesn't mean you're running, just not tied down."

"A man like you's got to have a reason to not want to be tied down. I know your sort."

"Who says I don't want it?"

Spruce stood up and poured out the last, cold inch of coffee from the bottom of his mug. "Thank you for your hospitality. I'll be moving on now."

"Look, when you win, I'll collect the money and we'll meet in town, you hear?"

"When I win?" A touch of a smile crept into Spruce's eye as he turned and strode into the darkness.

THE MORNING of the race was still and frozen, like a held breath. The course had been laid out—Laramie hadn't seen it, but Spruce had, and he said it would be easy enough. The cold weather suited his dogs too, making for hard, fast trail.

Nine drivers stood ready, trappers and freight runners and local men all, with a motley assortment of dogs. Spruce towered like a tree among them with his grim silence and his hood pushed back on his shoulders, showing his fair hair among the fur-lined hoods and graying hair. He checked his brake and crouched down on the runners, one hand on the handlebars as he reached with the other to check the lashing on his sled bag.

Laramie kept his eyes on the fellow in case he should look over to the crowd for him, but he never did.

"Teams on your marks!"

The dogs were barking, screaming almost, lunging in their harnesses. Slowly Spruce straightened, and with a shouted word, all but lost in the clamor, brought his dogs to the mark.

The starting gun sounded and the teams were away like a shot.

Laramie glanced once more out at the trampled snow and trudged back the way he had come. In an hour or so, the teams would be back around the hills and heading back into town for the finish, and standing around in the cold wouldn't help it go any faster.

"Laramie!"

Sergeant Nolan stood outside the outfitters, leaning against a post, smoking again.

"Sir." Laramie gave him a quiet salute, which Nolan returned briefly.

"You out to see the races too?"

"Yes sir, I am."

"It's a bit different from back home, ain't it?" Nolan smiled and scuffed the snow with his boot. "But the same things make a man tick, halfway around the world."

Laramie chuckled. "You bettin'?"

"Naw." Nolan shook his head and pulled his gloves back on. "Just making sure things stay peaceable on our end."

"Say, you want to step in for some coffee? I was going to wait this one out somewhere away from the wind. I ain't young anymore."

Nolan laughed. "Don't mind if I do."

ALMOST TWO HOURS LATER, as Laramie watched from the low-roofed porch of the Kaquom trading post, Spruce pulled into town alone, with a team as good as gold and fresh as snow.

THE NEXT MORNING, when the men had eaten and the camp was buttoned up for the morning, Laramie headed into town, his winnings folded in a fat wad in his coat pocket.

Nolan appeared from across the street, no longer wearing his green wool coat, but bundled in a new fur parka from the outfitters.

"Sir." Laramie saluted.

"Laramie, I hear you made out like a bandit."

"Well, sir, you know what they say about camp cooks. Looks like you placed a bet on the sly yourself?"

Nolan laughed. "Just doing some much needed trading."

"Say, have you seen Spruce?"

"Sure, heard he was at the Pick and Collarbone. Been holding offers at arm's length all morning. You better get to him fast."

"Will do, Sergeant."

Laramie stepped into the dim building, blinking as his eyes adjusted from the blinding glare of the snow. Spruce was leaning against the bar, fiddling with an empty glass. It was in his left hand, the one missing the fingers.

"For a man who doesn't drink, you spend a lot of time in the drinking house."

Spruce looked up. "There you are."

He held out his hand and Laramie took it firmly. "I have your cut."

"Excellent." Spruce pushed himself off of the bar and crossed the room to an out-of-the-way table.

Laramie slid into the chair across from him and counted out Spruce's share, plus a little extra.

"Look." Spruce folded up his cut but pulled the extra off. "We made a deal. I don't need favors."

"It's a gift. Knew a fellow once, a fine officer, reminded me of you."

"Oh?"

"But that was a long time ago. He was almost my age. Heard he died out on some far frontier."

"I see."

Quietly, Spruce folded up the remainder of the money and pocketed it. "Hanni?"

The girl was passing by. He hardly had to speak and she turned.

"Would you get us a pot of coffee? I could use something hot before I leave."

"Right away," she whispered.

"You leaving?"

"I'm heading up north, like I said I was." Spruce leaned back in his chair.

"That was before you changed your mind."

"About the one race, yes. Nothing else."

"With a pile like this, you don't need to trap."

Spruce laughed under his breath, a short, sad thing.

"No, I think I'm bound to follow the wind the rest of my life. Men like me, we don't settle and we can't."

"You said you had a stake outside Chegak."

"A stake isn't a home."

"It could be a start, boy."

Spruce fingered the edge of the table and didn't look up.

"Your coffee."

Spruce glanced up at the girl, and their gazes held just a moment longer than they should.

"Thanks."

She left, softly, and Spruce reached out to pour the coffee.

"Well, here's to our successful partnership." Laramie lifted his cup and held it out in a toast.

Spruce lifted his briefly and drank.

THEY FINISHED the pot and Spruce paid, leaving the money on the table.

It was quiet outside, moving on towards late morning. The street was empty.

"I guess this is where we part ways," said Spruce. "My dogs are hitched and waiting for me out by the lot."

"Good doing business, Spruce." Laramie held out his hand.

A smile lurked in Spruce's eyes as he took it. "Well, I still don't like the army much, but you're all right."

"So are you. Safe journey."

"And to you—wherever you go after this."

Spruce pulled the brim of his hat in farewell and started down the street.

IT WAS A COUPLE WEEKS LATER, while he was standing at the bar of the Pick and Collarbone watching the proprietor, Mr. Stone, pour his drink, that it struck him.

"That girl, Hanni—I haven't seen her in a week or two now."

"Oh, her." Mr. Stone glanced over his spectacles. "She left. Went home finally. Her father died some time back, left her a homestead twenty miles east of here. Poor as dirt she was, had years of debt racked up from doctors and her father's medicines, but she wouldn't sell."

"And?"

Mr. Stone shrugged. "Well, she came into some money. A whole pile. Don't know how…she hasn't got a living relative that I know of. And she certainly didn't have anything to bet with."

"Hm." With a slow nod, Laramie slid a coin across the bar.

"Will you need anything else?"

"Naw, this'll do me."

The room was full, loud and smoky, but no one saw Laramie raise his glass, as if to an invisible partner, and down it.

DEATH AT THE OVERFLOW

9

DEATH AT THE OVERFLOW

There were four missing. If it had been two, he might have let them break their fool necks. If it had been six, he'd have taken another man.

As it was, standing at the picket line, looking at the broken tethers, Rutter decided he'd go after the horses himself. It would be faster that way, no fool of a horse-boy spooking them off. He'd call and they'd come.

Besides, if he was quick about it, Captain Innes wouldn't have to know.

"Maki! Maki—lad, where are you?" It was hard for him to remember to treat her like a boy—now that he knew, it was plain as the nose on his face what she was, but he did his best to keep up the facade.

She ducked around the neck of one of the horses, her dark eyes making her look like a deer peering out of the woods.

"What is it?"

She wore the look she always wore when she spoke to him—solemn, almost displeased.

"Four horses are missing. I am taking a fifth and riding out to collect them. They won't be hard to track with the snow."

"Unless it snows again." She rubbed her hands off. "Do you think they went far?"

"No telling. They probably pulled loose early in the night. Anyway, I'm hoping I can track them. I—don't suppose you'd lend me your dog? It'll be a mite quicker that way."

Her solemn expression turned reproachful, but she snapped her fingers for her dog.

She crouched down beside the massive, wolf-like creature and spoke to him in her language, quietly. Then, easy as that, he padded over to Rutter.

"He will find them, faster than you could." She said it in a strange way that left Rutter turning her words round in his head, trying to figure out if she had just agreed with him or insulted him.

He didn't have the time to waste on it.

He hefted a saddle onto a spare bay, cinched it tight, and fit the bridle over its head. Like a clock, not even thinking, just moving swift and sure.

"Mind you button up," Maki said in that same strange tone. "You might freeze. To death," she added after a pause, as if he needed the clarification.

"Sure, sure."

He thrust his foot into the stirrup and dropped solidly into the saddle. "If anyone asks, you tell them where I've gone, mind?"

Maki nodded.

Ten to one no one would even notice his absence. There'd been so much coming and going today between the camp and the shore where the whale was being harvested that no one knew where anyone was, really.

He wheeled, the horse tossing its head in mild protest, and rode out of camp in the direction of the tracks.

THE HOOFPRINTS WANDERED. Like every witless horse, they had picked at this and that under the snow, skittered at night sounds, and churned up snow and dirt in their progress.

Rutter whistled to Iki, who had begun to stray. The whistle caught his attention, but he wasn't inclined to obey. Perhaps he hadn't needed the dog—these horses had made it look like a herd of cattle had come through.

He stopped the horse and peered into the frozen mist that hung over the rolling ground for a sign of his quarry.

Nothing.

Iki came back, seeming at last to be interested in tracking. He followed the hoofprints, his tail swinging low, his nose pressed to the frozen ground.

"Hup!" Rutter urged the horse forward with a slap of the reins.

The land unfolded before him, a rising and falling ground not unlike sea-waves, foamy with caps of snow. In the far distance, lacing the horizon, stood purple-blue mountains.

They'd been over hills and bits of cliffs, forests and valleys, but this—this was prime land, even if it was too cold. His horse snorted, enjoying the liberty to run.

And Iki, long-limbed, his tongue lolling happily, was keeping easy pace.

Rutter had the sudden, unpleasant thought that perhaps

all the wolves in this land could do that—keep pace with a running horse.

Below them, hidden in ice that seemed pushed over the banks by sheer excess, ran a thin river. It was as if someone had reached down and traced a line across the land with their finger.

It might be slick, but it looked easy enough to cross if one was careful. The tracks trailed off, and he guessed the horses had wandered up and down to find a crossing.

Iki stopped.

"Come on!" Rutter called, but the dog only looked at him and started to trot south, his nose to the icy ground.

"Come on, Iki!" Rutter cupped his gloved hands to his mouth and shouted, but the dog kept going.

He urged the horse forward and the world tilted.

The ice met him with a hard thud. Pain spread across the side of his head in a dull, mean ache.

Fool horse. Bloody fool horse.

The ice was singing. It was a high, tight sort of whine, the sound of it spinning gently around until he could not keep track any longer....

RUTTER WOKE from darkness to a shaky, pale daylight and the warm rough tongue of a dog in his face.

His head pounded, his senses cutting in and out. The dog's breath was reviving him—it smelled awful. He sat up and looked around at the pale, desolate ice.

The horse was on its side, six inches of water welling around it, growing. He dragged himself to his feet, and Iki calmly backed up, as if he had been waiting for the man to stand.

Rutter skirted the horse slowly, icy water seeping into his boots. He felt along one leg that was swelling already—it was broken, right above the fetlock. The horse was ruined.

What luck.

He muttered curses to himself as he checked the powder in his gun. Of course he'd had to bring another horse out, lose it for good.

It couldn't be helped, but he hated what he had to do now—hated it worse than anything else in this rough, wild land.

He took aim, steadying his gaze, which was trying to swim away from him, and fired.

Poor old thing would be all right now.

He wiped his nose on his sleeve. It was getting colder, and his head ached something powerful. The hoofprints led away southeast.

"Come on, Iki." He whistled to the dog and started across the cold, crunching ground.

This time Iki followed without hesitation.

How much time had passed, Rutter couldn't quite figure. He only knew he had been walking a powerful long time, and his head hurt.

It had begun to snow again. Not only would he lose the horse tracks, but his own bootprints would be swallowed up in the new snow and no one would be able to track him, either.

"What a mess," he muttered. Iki looked up and wagged his tail.

Dusk fell sometime after Rutter could no longer feel his feet. He stumbled and fell twice, Iki hovering around in an attempt to be helpful. Finally he decided that nothing more could be gained.

He had to start a fire and make camp or he'd die.

There wasn't much to start a fire with—some dry grass that the powder snow hadn't dampened, a piece of a log he found by the river (the tiresome thing had followed him, twisting round on itself and ending up due south of him). Not far from the banks, he set up camp and started his fire.

When the fire was going, small but better than nothing, he pulled his boots off and stuck his frozen feet as close to the flames as he dared. A couple of his toes were waxy white (Maki had warned him about that happening to his face), so he took his gloves off, leaned forward, and laid his hands over the toes to help warm them slowly.

Iki yawned, perked his ears briefly at the darkness to the north, and laid his head on his paws with a sigh.

The snow came and went with the clouds—sometimes Rutter could see the pinprick of stars above the orange light of the fire, sometimes the snow blotted it out, swirling and dancing in the thick darkness.

He was cold. Powerful cold. And he knew that if he didn't stay warm, he'd fall asleep and never wake up.

He couldn't risk that.

"C'mere." He stretched out beside the fire and put his arms around the dog's neck. Iki pressed against him, pleased. After all, the dog often settled between him and Maki of nights. He was accustomed to this.

They lay together for some time, the fire crackling cheerily, the dog breathing contentedly, the darkness beyond them quiet and still.

But the chill continued to advance. He might not know

much about this wild land, but he could tell when the temperature was plummeting.

Maybe this was the end.

The sparks coursed upwards, a thin comfort in the breath-crackling cold around him. He couldn't even take a breath without covering his mouth.

Lights flashed in his eyes. He saw shapes moving beyond the firelight, but when he looked again, they were gone.

He pulled closer to the fire, causing Iki to scramble to his feet. He was so cold he could lay almost in the embers, and still they wouldn't warm him fast enough.

The fire was dimming. He revived enough to stir it, poke it towards life, but it only fought briefly and gave up.

He was losing the fire. He would be next.

"Iki!" He snapped numb fingers for the dog. But Iki was staring northwards again. He took a stiff step in that direction and stopped.

"Iki, come here."

The dog looked back at him once and then sprang forward, into the night.

"Iki! *Iki!*" But the dog was gone. His voice echoed back in his mind, too many times.

So this was it. This was the end of old Rutter, nearly-demoted head groom for Captain Innes of the Army of the Northern Frontier.

The Northern Frontier had been too much. Too much for Rutter, the man who tried but hadn't amounted to anything.

It was a strange thing. A day or two ago, he would have said that he had done well for himself in life. Now, here, he felt awful empty and lonely.

He didn't want it to end here.

GOLDEN LIGHT POURED into his eyes, along with the long, grim face of Drucker.

If he'd held any hopes of waking to paradise, Drucker's face shot that dead.

"Just in the nick," Drucker declared to someone outside the halo of light. The tall doctor straightened, rubbed his brown and gray beard thoughtfully. "Give him that coffee, Laramie. It'll warm him up. Thaw him out slow and start that fire up."

Rutter tried to sit up. His mouth felt frozen shut. He wanted to talk, but no words were coming.

"Easy now, bub." Drucker's firm hand pushed him back. "Don't go trying to kill yourself now that we're here. I might just let you."

A laugh made it out where words wouldn't, but it didn't even sound like much of a laugh in Rutter's ears.

"It was that doggone wolf-dog." Drucker dusted snow off his hands and stood. "Came and met us halfway. I've got to hand it to you, you sure got yourself plumb in the middle of nowhere."

From the ground beside Drucker's boots, he looked a hundred feet tall. No wonder the men were afraid of him.

"An hour later, and—" Drucker shrugged, and the firelight flared up the side of his face as he regarded Rutter with a face as blank as stone.

"Well. You'll live."

RANSOM'S LAST STAND

10

RANSOM'S LAST STAND

They tell you, when you join the army—when you sit at those rigid desks at the academy, studying the brilliant strategists of the past—that one day you will reach your impossible choice.

Twenty-three years, and I've reached mine.

THE MORNING LIGHT WAS PEACEFUL, cheerful even, slanting across my field desk littered with papers and books, the field manuals I kept with me always. I remember the moment with startling clarity.

A knock came on the tent post—better than nothing. The men tried to give me warning.

I had arrived at the camp in Carthena to take the place of Captain Winfield on the previous day; ever since I had successfully withdrawn the army of the Northern Frontier without casualties, I had found myself strategically assigned to diplomatically sensitive situations—in this case, the Irylia-Gadarone border dispute. Some sixty years ago, Irylia's nearest neighbor to the south had allied with our sworn enemies in a naval spat, and ever since, the ancient dispute over the border regions had come back into play. The claims were as tired as they were old, but the whole affair still managed to be a touchy piece of politics.

I shrugged on my green jacket with the gold buttons and told the man to enter. He was an orderly, young and bursting with apprehension in every nerve.

"Sir." The orderly saluted.

"Go ahead." I was arranging my inkstand, taming my papers from the night before that had cost an entire precious candle.

"The scouting party was captured—the entire patrol. Word came from the Gadarone headquarters that they have them and want a ransom."

"Is the messenger waiting?" My head hurt and my mind was running with the implications. Any dead? Wounded? Is there information they will try to get out of the men? Anything that would be fatal to us if someone talked?

"No. He did not wait for a reply."

"I see."

It was six men, the scouting patrol I had sent out under the cover of night to discern our position. They were the best I had. I don't know if I'll ever know why it failed, on this night out of the dozens they had managed without incident.

"How much do they want?"

The man seemed to be working up his courage to reply. I braced myself. Of course things had to be complicated.

"Fourteen thousand, sir."

The amount almost didn't register at first. It was too much for a scouting patrol. It was a captain's ransom or a king's nephew's ransom—not what you ask for a band of scouts.

"Did they say when they want it by?"

"Dawn tomorrow, or they start to work on our boys."

"Well." I ran my hand across my forehead. I needed coffee. "That gives me a little time. Anything else?"

"No, sir."

"Dismissed."

"Sir." He ducked out.

The truth was, it was probably all a lie. They had probably started pressing our men for information almost immediately. The high demand bought them time—there was no way I had access to that kind of money in the field.

They were six good men.

I dropped my head into my hands and stared at the worn field desk below me. Seventeen years it had served me well—a present from Captain Sutton, after my old desk was lost with a supply wagon in a river out near Forks Gap, half a world away.

Every campaign has moments like this, but this time, I had to be frank with myself. I didn't know what I was going to do.

Spring had taken over the trees in buds, but the air was still chilled with the leftovers of winter. I wore my full winter uniform to meet the parley delegation—an officer, an escort, and six hooded prisoners under guard.

It was dirty of them to bring the men out. They knew as well as I that I did not have the fourteen thousand.

The officer stepped forward to meet me, the two of us leaving our escorts to stand face to face in the middle ground. He was young, with an affected brown mustache and hair that certainly would not be allowed in my camp.

"Captain Alonso LeGrande of the Third Light Horse," he greeted with a stiff salute.

"Captain John Ransom." I returned it politely, with an effort.

"Name of Ransom—did they send you on purpose?" He laughed at his own joke.

I let him laugh himself into awkward silence.

"Did you bring the fourteen thousand?" he demanded, when he realized I would not share in his joke.

"I think you know there's only one answer to that."

"And I think you'll regret that." He turned around, snapping his fingers to one of the men behind him.

They jerked the hood off of the first man in line—Hawthorne. The side of his face turned toward me was discolored with bruises and dried blood. He kept his eyes down and dead as stone. I think he had an inkling of the position I was in and didn't want to make my job more painful.

When a man does a thing like that, it makes things easier in one way, but far harder in another.

"You said you were going to wait." I let the reproach in my voice stand out. Not surprise, but reproach.

Captain LeGrande gave a sniff of laughter. "And here I thought you called a parley to actually barter."

Hawthorne looks at me finally, a brief, swift look. He's always been a quick lad, slim, boy-faced—the sort that doesn't stand out until he's run circles around the others and you have to reframe your opinion of him.

He's asking a question in that look, and I wish I could give him an answer.

"I came to offer you an alternative, as it seems that you haven't had much need to bargain in your years of service."

He stiffened. The implication of his inexperience had struck home, though I hadn't meant it that way. His youth might be useful to me after all.

"And what is that?"

"We have in our charge fifteen foot-soldiers of your company. To trade them for our six men is nearly a three-to-one exchange."

He snorted. "And would you demand fourteen thousand for fifteen foot-soldiers?"

"I would not demand fourteen thousand for a scouting party."

"There is no deal. I thought you would be a more reasonable man, with these men and the information of your camp on the line, but you have exceeded the hour by which we required our demand."

"The pretense is not needed, Captain LeGrande. You and I both know you were not constrained by that."

I saluted in farewell and called my escort off. Nothing would be gained by further talk with that green colt of an officer.

THE COMMANDER of the entire southern front rode in that evening. He was a tall, slightly sallow man with a gentle face and voice, but eyes that I never quite trusted.

He settled in my camp chair with a glass of wine, and I sat across from him on my camp chest.

"You are Captain John Ransom?"

"That is correct."

"Formerly of the Army of the Northern Frontier, I

understand, and of the company that went into the far north?"

"I commanded the return division."

"After Captain Innes's tragic death. He was a fine officer."

I cradled my own cup of untouched wine in my hands. "He was."

Commander Talbot shook his head sadly and took a sip of his wine as if in salute. Then he set it down and folded his hands. "It seems clear that they want something besides money or an exchange of prisoners."

"They want a fight."

"And the information those six men have. They are a risk to us every moment they are alive."

"I know those men well. They won't talk."

"All six?"

I let silence stand between us a moment. Not because I doubt, but because that question doesn't deserve answering right away.

I do know those six well. Hawthorne, who is steel under a gentle face; Thomas, who is like an unbroken colt but would die for his cause; Collins, who is as stubborn as rock; Patrick, who has already proved in battle he's no coward—I could think of a dozen reasons to trust each one.

"Beyond a doubt."

"Hmm." His tone gave such a flippant response to my conviction that I felt as if he had slapped me. "There's really no telling."

"Sir. With respect, I have led men for twenty-three years over some of the most unforgiving terrain and into some of the deadliest combat Irylia has faced in a hundred years. This is not these men's first trial."

Commander Talbot nodded sagely. "Then they will understand the sacrifices that need to be made."

"Sir?" I didn't want him to clarify, but I had no choice.

"Send in a sharpshooter. If they're dead, there's no collateral."

Years of service and practice saved me from the scathing answer I nearly gave. I cleared my throat.

"That is the short-term solution. In the long run, all it will do is prove to LeGrande that we cannot keep our word and that he has backed us into a corner. And as he clearly cannot keep his word, I would not advise giving him reason to justify it or to claim that he does have us pinned."

"The enemy already knows that."

"They do not, sir. The commanding officer is young and green. He is making demands because he thinks he can. If we wait him out, cooler heads on his side will prevail. We can demand to talk to a superior officer, even as I am doing with you."

"We don't have that kind of time."

"It will only take another day. Commander Redamé is half a day's ride down their line, I know it."

"Six men, Ransom." He swore. "Six scouts. You cannot endanger the border of Irylia for them."

"I am endangering nothing. I asked for another day, that's all."

"Another day for them to come up with excuses, to exploit our towns, to torture those men for information. Do you not see the need for haste?"

"Better another day with small losses than stumble into a full-fledged war. Rushing into a decision and breaking our word will not help the peace efforts. And I was led to understand that peace was paramount."

"Are you questioning me, captain?"

"No, I am simply informing you of the facts as they stand."

"The Gadarones are not some northern *savets* or cattle-dealing nomads. They are quick and underhanded, and they will press their advantage. Tell them the money will come day after next and put them off their guard. Then send a man in covertly to shoot them. I can arrange for one if you do not have a sharpshooter at your disposal. Thus we put a swift end to their attempts to gain the upper hand and we show them that they cannot play games."

"Sir—"

"No, Captain Ransom. I will not permit you to argue."

I took a deep breath, steadied myself before I answered. "I am not giving an order to lie to the enemy in parley or to shoot my own men."

Commander Talbot leaned deeper into my chair. "I am not giving you a choice."

"It is not right, sir."

"Perhaps I have not made myself clear." He could make his voice uncannily gentle when he chose. "If you delay or disobey me in this, you are through, Ransom. An immediate dishonorable discharge."

I was on my feet, he on his. I don't even remember how we got there.

"I hear." My heart pounded in my ears. I was so angry I could hardly get the words out.

"Remember that."

He pushed out of the tent, and I stood there until the sounds of his escort mounting up and riding away were gone.

It was silent, and the cold spring air pushed the tent flap open, gently.

"Orderly?"

"Sir?"

"First light, I want a messenger sent under flag of truce to Captain LeGrande. Tell him I want to parley."

THE WIND WAS strong and fretful that morning, hard on the face and the hands and the tents, drying up the spring mud and the melting snow. LeGrande was suspicious at my demand to talk to one of my men, but I promised no tricks and no lies.

It was Treacher they appointed as spokesman—the only one who could lie to me. He didn't exactly smile, but his expression was easy and reassuring, despite the burn mark I saw inside his shirt collar.

"Captain Ransom," he began in a quiet voice, so they couldn't catch his words, "we're all right. Don't listen to them. This is important, you know that. Just don't listen to them, sir."

I stared into his eyes, trying to find a crack in his front. But he was ready for me.

"Where is Corporal Thomas?"

I had demanded that they all be present, but there was only five of them. Thomas's lanky form was conspicuously absent.

Treacher looked me dead in the eye, and I knew those words, at least, were no lie. "I can't tell you, sir. For the men's sake, I can't."

He raised his voice for the benefit of the guard,

standing behind him a couple paces. "We need that fourteen thousand, sir."

"We are working on it. Hold until we can get it."

"Yes, sir."

I let Corporal Thomas's absence go and tried a different tack, under my breath. I needed him to be honest with me. "You are not all right."

This quiet reproach took him by surprise, and I saw the crack in his front for just a moment. The edge of his mouth twitched.

I lowered my voice. "I have orders to open fire on you tonight. I need the truth, now."

"We'll be all right, but we need two days." They had a plan, then. "If you can stall them two days…."

"I can't promise you two days, but I can give you one. The rest of today and all night."

The wind knifed between us, blowing our coats, stilling our voices. We could not risk it carrying to the guard.

When it died down, Treacher was ready for me. "Then one day it is."

The lying front was gone. His eyes met mine as they took him away, the look clear as day. *We won't let you down, sir.*

And I wouldn't let them down either.

THEY ALWAYS TELL YOU, when you join the army, when you train to be an officer, that one day you will reach your impossible choice.

Twenty-three years, and I've reached mine. But it's not a choice. Not anymore. Since the day I took oath, everything I've done has been for the men.

I'm not about to change that.

. . .

I STAY UP THAT NIGHT, watching the camp, listening to the change of the pickets, packing my trunk. Keeping guard over every man's coming and going. Protecting my boys, for the last time, from afar. Morning dawns under a heavy frost, and my orderly brings in the coffee just after daybreak.

"I am sorry, sir. I didn't want to disturb you, as you were up late."

"It is nothing." I rub my forehead wearily. "I didn't sleep."

"If I may say, sir, you don't look well."

"I am well enough."

"Do you need anything else, sir?"

"Saddle my horse. I want to inspect the camp."

I RIDE THE LINES, steeped in gray mist, for the last time. I salute the men as they salute me. Those trusting faces. I'm doing it for them. I look in on the wounded, stop a few minutes to chat with my supplies officer, a good friend. I laugh, I talk with them, I look on the sights that had been my life for the last twenty-three years.

Commander Talbot arrives just after midmorning. I have been expecting him for the last hour. I'm nearly packed, neatening the last stacks of papers, laying them in my satchel.

"Is it done?"

I can't tell from his face what he expects to hear from me. From the absence of papers on my field desk, he should guess.

"No, sir. It is not done."

His face goes still. "You would defy me?"

"It was not done in defiance of you in particular, sir. Only the order." I'm through—I may as well say what I wish.

"Pack your things. I want you gone before the day is out. There may even be a court-martial."

I raise the last stack of my papers to him before settling them in the overfilled satchel. "You know where my home is. Send the discharge papers there. I won't go anywhere."

He's still reeling; his face is flushing red.

"What were you thinking?"

"I was thinking of the men." I shut my satchel and pull the buckles tight like the cinch on a saddle. It's been years since the thing closed properly.

"The men? A slow death for a fast one? Our secrets spilled to the enemy?"

"I wasn't just thinking of those six."

I duck my head under the strap of the satchel and head for the door. "Have them send my things along later. No need to stay any longer, sir."

I salute, for the last time, and he holds me at attention deliberately longer than is natural.

When he finally dismisses me, my orderly has my horse ready. There's an uncertain crowd gathering, but they part for me.

I wish I could tell them it was all right. But a man can't see the future. I worked for their best interest as long as it was my power; now I have to leave them and hope Providence will be kind.

I ride away, up past the lines, to the barren hills well beyond the army lines. It's only then that I turn—I only let myself look back once—and see the white specks, like snowflakes, that house my men. It was for them. Everything was for them.

I have cried seldom in my years of service. But I hide my face in my hand and I cry now.

REGRETS. That's what they said I'd have. The next morning, the following week, in my old age. It has been only a month, but so far, I have not felt it. Sorrow, yes. Wishing the circumstances had been different, to be sure. But not a hint of regret for my actions.

Men are alive who otherwise wouldn't be—thousands of lives, possibly, though it never does to count could-have-beens. As it is, the only one who lost was me, and only from a strategic standpoint. What is a dishonorable discharge, loss of pension, against the lives of my men? It stings, but I can be content with that.

My dog starts up, barking, and I get up, see three men coming through the gate, up the stone path to my door.

The first is Commander Harkness, the army's best officer of the last quarter-century; the second is a desk commander I know by face only; and the third is Hawthorne.

His face has healed, except for a brownish line where the worst of it was.

"Hush," I rebuke the dog softly, and she backs away as I open the door.

Commander Harkness clears his throat. "Captain Ransom." He's carrying a creamy white envelope, sealed with red wax.

"Just John Ransom," I correct him. "Will you come in?"

"No, thank you. We simply wished to deliver this." He

hands me the envelope. "And with it, the thanks of Irylia."

I open the envelope—with Hawthorne standing in front of me, I can guess the contents. I skim over the fine, black handwriting. A promotion, expungement of the dishonorable discharge.

"Change your mind?" I don't look up, but I can't keep the irony out of my voice.

"Your discharge was hasty, though your disobedience regrettable. As it turns out, when Commander Talbot's orders were discharged the following night, the hostages were already gone. They turned up a week later, all six, with full positions on the enemy's lines and a good deal of classified information. As you probably heard, the Gadarones conceded the land they seized."

I look up, only at Hawthorne. He's smiling that small, boyish smile of his.

I fold the paper up, return it to the envelope, hold it out. "Thank you, but I cannot accept this."

"Now Cap—Mr. Ransom. Please reconsider. The army, the country is in your debt. If that was not clear, you saved thousands of lives by your decision. To have killed those men would have been disastrous."

"It was clear." I straighten my shoulders. "And I made my decision, a month ago. I stood by it then and I stand by it now. Circumstances don't change that."

Commander Harkness takes the envelope quietly. "I understand." He gives me an almost apologetic nod.

He turns to leave, hesitates, and then holds out his hand. "I'd be honored."

I accept it and his grip is warm.

He and the other commander leave, but Hawthorne

lingers. I wait, we both wait, until the other two are beyond the gate.

"Captain, I speak for all of us—we boys are grateful." He clears his throat and goes on. "I know the risks of being a soldier. It's not that, but—I have a son, and Thomas does too, and we—we all had wives to go home to. I'm just saying, not every man would have done that for us. And we're grateful."

"I did it for all the men."

"Yes, but that doesn't change it. A thousand lives or six, you didn't hesitate."

I shake my head. "It's something many officers would do."

"No, sir. I disagree. It's easier to face down an enemy's gun than to defy one of your own."

He reaches into his pocket.

"The boys and I—they gave us this, after we got back. But we're all agreed, it's for you."

He presses a small box into my hand and hurries away up the path, leaving me alone in the twilight.

I do not open the box until he is gone. A folded paper lies on top, and it reads: *It is not the mark of a man's character how he stands when he stands with his companions, but rather how he stands when he is alone. —From grateful men.*

Irylia's highest honor—the medal for valor—lies beneath it.

TUSIK'S FOLLY

11

TUSIK'S FOLLY

Word passed from mouth to mouth: Girdwood Falmouth will win the cup. All of Heart's End was abuzz with the word. For two years, bad luck had plagued him—his horse Rosie Ring had pulled up lame at the three-quarter mark last year, and the year before that, Copper's Sun had lost by a nose to Whiskey Blackthorne after a stray dog wandered onto the track.

But this year, Falmouth came to town with a big, long-limbed horse. Gray and mouse-colored, it had the look of a carthorse, but it stepped quick and shy, like a thoroughbred.

"Tusik's Folly," Falmouth announced, slapping the tall shoulder beside him. "Her mum was a pacer, her pa an army stud."

"And where'd you get your claws on her?" asked Butch, the resident barman, odds-maker when the time of year came for the cup.

A wry dimple appeared in the corner of the man's mouth. He smoothed back his thick brown hair. "Traded her for three plew of lynx and Copper's mother. Hated to do it."

A trickle of disbelieving laughter wound through the crowd, too weak to touch Falmouth. His gray-blue eyes shone up at the filly.

"Now, if'n you'll excuse me." He reached out an arm toward the crowd as if to push them back. "She's a mite touchy around new folks."

A single cluck of his tongue and she followed him, lamblike, her head almost upon his shoulder, her body rippling like a tiger's.

"Falmouth's Filly will win the cup," breathed Butch, his broad head shaking dumbly.

THE MAP LAY on the center table of Butch's saloon, secured by three map pins and someone's bone-handled pocket knife.

"Pretty course this year," one of the regulars drawled around the thick, cheap cigar in his mouth. "Got a lot of wild land and some creek crossin' too."

"Figure the fancy-breds will break up on the creek bed? That's not easy crossin'."

"Not likely." Whiskey Blackthorne snuffed his cigar out against his glass of gin, leaving ash on the table. He dragged his long boots off the chair they were soiling and pulled his long frame up. He moved like a snake—lazy, until you crossed him. "You see, even though the course crosses the creek bed twice, it's all of a few strides for the leggy ones."

"You would say that," said Morgan, a man with a face like weathered leather. "Your own's one of thet type."

"Does that change anything?" Whiskey tilted his head back, his voice a purr.

"Some might say that." Butch was granted immunity by the fact that he had a choke-hold on the only legal pure in town. "But I say let the horses speak for themselves on cup day. No sense in starting fights now."

He poured a straight whiskey and gave the tray a push. "Mollie, take those to the gentlemen, will you?"

Mollie, the slight girl at the counter, dressed in somber black up to her neck, took the tray without a word.

"I intend to win, third year straight." Whiskey leaned back and smiled at Butch. His eyes lit on Mollie's raven hair. "And when I do, this young lady will put off her mourning, once and for all."

The girl forced a smile onto her face. "That may be so, but not until after the cup. I was very clear, wasn't I?"

"Oh, you were. No fear—it'll come soon enough."

Mollie stiffened and set the drinks down, taking up the empty glasses quickly.

The door swung open and all eyes went naturally to the newcomer. Girdwood Falmouth stood wreathed in the gold light, squinting a little.

"Whatsa matter, Fal?" Morgan gestured with a weather-beaten hand. "Come on in here. Map's all set out."

Without a word, Falmouth shut the door behind him. He passed by the men and the table, going to the counter where Butch was drying dishes. "I'm putting in my share now."

He drew a packet from his thin coat and laid two gold nuggets, three pinches of dust, and a silver earring into the pottery bowl.

"This is the champion's claim." Butch held out a broad

hand as if to push it back. "You best take a look at the map before you be setting down anything like that."

"This is my share," came the quiet reply.

"Very well."

"You just put in the champion's share?" Whiskey stood up, hooking his thumbs in his pockets. "Them's fighting words from a man who hasn't been able to close the deal."

"Seen my filly?"

"Sure, I seen her. You must think a lot of that nag to be matching up against me like this."

"I'm bettin' on it."

A slow grin spread across Whiskey's face. "And we'll see who's right."

"We will." Falmouth leaned back against the counter and rested his elbows on it. "I'll be signing my name now, Butch."

Butch shrugged his broad shoulders. "Mollie, fetch the pen and ink, will you?"

Silently, Mollie left the room.

One of the old regulars pulled a cigar from his teeth. "Hey, Falmouth, you should come take a gander at the course. You'll need to know it if that filly of yourn'll have a fool's chance."

"Or a folly's chance," said a tenderfoot with an over-raucous laugh, garnering a few scattered laughs.

Falmouth sauntered over, leaning very quietly over the table.

He rubbed a week's worth of fine stubble as he looked at the map, his thin, large-jointed finger tracing the course.

"Fine course," he said softly. "Finest yet."

Mollie was back. She cleared her throat gently, and Falmouth pulled back with a brief, respectful glance.

"Thanks."

"She's claimed," Whiskey smirked over his shoulder. "Any man touches her, I'll snap him like a twig."

If the comment was meant for Falmouth, he did not seem to hear. He took the pen and signed his name bold and thick, the "f" in Falmouth twisting like a salmon breaching out of the water.

WHISKEY PUSHED OPEN the livery stable door, letting the light of his lantern flood the aisleway and illuminate the spare figure of Girdwood Falmouth, who was stroking Folly's head.

"What kind of stunt was that back there?"

"Stunt?" Falmouth's shoulders tightened, but as he turned, there was no concern in his face.

"The champion's share."

"I have never answered to you, Whiskey. And today ain't the day."

"Figured I'd find you out here." Whiskey leaned against the ladder to the loft and cocked his head. "On'y place you seem to be."

Falmouth turned away and resumed stroking Folly.

"I wasn't done talking." Whiskey pushed himself off with his shoulder. "I said I don't like what you done."

"Can't undo it."

"By gur, you can." Whiskey pulled back his long coat, showing a brace of pistols. "And you can right now."

Falmouth only glanced at him. "If you keep on showing those pistols to everyone who doesn't suit your style, you just may find yourself six feet under."

Whiskey leaned close. "Is that a threat?"

Falmouth gave a thin smile. "Not from me."

Whiskey let his coat fall back over his pistols. "They say never trust a man from Arislet who's too quiet. He's likely to be hiding a knife."

"Do they really?"

Whiskey's hand shot out and caught the other man's collar. "It'd be mighty hard to race tomorrow if I snapped you in half."

"True." Falmouth smiled again and let his head rest against the wall of the stable. "But I reckon you'd lose your spot too, seeing as you're the only one with enough horse in the stakes to fear Tusik's Folly."

Whiskey's hand loosened its grip slightly.

"Now, see here." Falmouth fixed him with his gray-blue gaze. "It'd be mighty rotten to settle it between the two of us and not the horseflesh. What's more, I'll make you a solid bet."

"Be ready to lose."

A glint came into Falmouth's eyes. "I mean to get what I set out to get. Whatever it takes. That's why I'm willing to gamble."

"You think you can play the game dirtier than me? That's not your style, Falmouth."

Falmouth shrugged. "When a man is desperate, he does what he must."

"You didn't hardly look over the course out there."

"Didn't need to."

"You saying you got another way?"

"I didn't say nothing."

Whiskey's grip tightened again and he shook the man hard. "You tell me what you're up to."

"I'm only saying if you don't see me behind you, you

better run for the finish like the devil was on your tail. I'll tell you that much, in fair sport."

"If I find you've cheated me, I am going to put you in bed for weeks."

Falmouth smiled. "Then there's a lot at stake."

"What's the bet?"

"Five to one. And we lose something precious to us."

Whiskey took a step closer. This was what he lived off—gold and gouging enemies where it hurt.

"What do you have in mind?"

Falmouth gave a sly smile. "That girl is putting you off. To see her do it once more is good enough for me."

"Mollie? Done. For you, I want Tusik's Folly."

"Folly?" Falmouth's voice almost failed him.

"I will take no less." Whiskey held out his hand in challenge. "No hard feelings?"

After a slight hesitation, Falmouth took it. "No hard feelings. But what if we both lose? All bets off?"

Whiskey smiled. "You know no horse in town has half the speed of my Red River."

"Very well."

As Falmouth began to pull his hand back, Whiskey's clamped down hard and he pulled Falmouth close. "But you best run fast, because I intend to ruin you."

Falmouth forced a smile. "I'd better win, then."

THE MORNING WAS cold and pale, mist clinging to the ground as thick as mess-house stew. A stillness held sway over the town, broken only by horses' whinnies, tight whispers, and the sharp, short bark of a dog.

Time ticked down to the race, and all Heart's End held its breath.

Whiskey Blackthorn was there already, his tall Red River chewing the bit nervously, letting out a bugle now and then. Whiskey smiled to himself from time to time, caught up in some private dream—probably a wedding with Mollie and his fist connecting smoothly with the jaw of Girdwood Falmouth.

Five other horses joined Red River on the field: a couple chasers, an ex-army mount, and two imports from the low lands. Last of all came Falmouth with Folly towering over him, throwing her head, dancing a little on her forelegs.

"Morning," he greeted the villagers as he passed.

"Morning," they replied, their eyes following him.

He stood without a word as the race marshal tied colors to his upper arm and Folly's headstall. The devil-may-care stubble was gone, and his face was as fresh as a boy's. He wore a gray cap, but no coat against the cold—only a forest green vest over his shirtsleeves.

If he was nervous, he didn't show it.

"Good luck." The marshal slapped Falmouth's shoulder.

"Thank you."

He led Folly to one side, a little distance from the other horses, and pulled himself into the light racing saddle to wait.

Whispers hovered and swirled around the watching crowd. Whiskey had spread the word of his bet. Half the town believed it. The other half refused to believe that Falmouth would risk putting a horse of his into the hands of a man like Whiskey—it wasn't to be thought of.

"Horses to the line!"

Like specters appearing out of the mist, the horses came, head-tossing, prancing, plodding. There was a moment of silence, holding of breaths.

The pistol was raised. The riders crouched over the necks of their mounts.

"Go!" The crack cut the still morning, and like an earthquake, the horses were off.

THE HORSES PUSHED their necks into racing up the hills, the shouts of the riders mingling with the thunder of the hooves. Seven miles lay ahead of them: creek crossings and tundra, timberland, and finally a flat run back to Heart's End. The weak were weeded out by the time Red River reached the tundra.

At the timber, Whiskey checked under his arm, but he saw only Tom Yarrow on his black. Falmouth and Folly must have found another way through.

By the time Whiskey gained open ground again, he had left Yarrow behind. Still he did not see Falmouth.

I'm only saying if you don't see me behind you, you better run for the finish like the devil was on your tail.

Two miles left. Enough time for treachery.

"Come on, Red!" He slashed his crop across the horse's hindquarters, dug in the spurs.

Red put forth a fresh burst of speed.

THE TOWN WAS FAST APPROACHING—THE outer steads and fishing equipment, the boats tied on the river. They appeared and whipped past, landmark by landmark, showing him the way to victory.

Still, Falmouth and his Folly were nowhere in sight.

"It's Blackthorne and Red!" came the shout. Wherever Falmouth was, he was behind.

They shot across the line like a bolt of lightning, a blur in the mist. Cheers drowned out the sound of hooves as the rest of the pack materialized out of the mist, just outside town.

Whiskey raised his crop over his head in victory, letting the reins fall onto his horse's neck. Red River came to a sobbing halt. He had run the race of his life.

"Fine fellow!" cried the marshal as he took Red's sweat-soaked head. "Congratulations on a third win, Blackthorne!"

Whiskey Blackthorne grinned and looked around. "Where is he?"

"Falmouth?"

One of the judges looked around. "Where is Falmouth?"

"Not here yet." Yarrow circled back. "I took second, solid."

"Did he have trouble? Did you see him fall?"

"Can't say I did."

"No matter, I'm cleaning him out for good," said Whiskey. "Take Red—he's spent. I'll ride my Folly around for the next few days, I reckon!"

He laughed, and a few of the rougher characters joined him.

The judge took the horse's head without a word and led the horse off, limping.

Butch the bartender was surrounded by frenzied men,

some angry, some elated. "Now, now! Back down, back down!"

Whiskey waded through the crowd. "Hey, Butch, you seen Mollie?"

"She's at the saloon, I reckon. She stayed behind to do the dishes."

"Reckon I'll go propose. She can't refuse, by her own word."

Butch's face turned a shade darker. "Morgan, come take the betting tables! I'm going with Whiskey."

He fell in step with Whiskey. "Now then, don't you think it's a bit soon? Go hash it out with Falmouth first. Mollie's a sensitive gal, being in mourning and all."

"Once I have Mollie at my side, I'll go make sure Falmouth pays everything he owes!" Whiskey grinned with pleasure at the thought.

The saloon was dark as he stomped in.

"Mollie! Your man has come!"

No answer.

"Mollie!"

Feet came pounding up from the porch outside.

"Whiskey, Whiskey!" It was a race judge. "Falmouth didn't cross the finish! Lev says no one saw him after the third hill!"

"No one?" He was only half listening. "Mollie! Blast you, gal, where'd you git to?"

"Saints preserve us!" uttered Butch from the counter in the tones of a dying man.

"What?" Whiskey tore over to the bar.

Mollie's black mourning clothes were folded behind the counter. Beside them, forgotten, lay a crumpled paper, worn as if had been read a hundred times.

With shaking hands, Whiskey smoothed it out against the countertop. An oath burst from him, long and fervent.

The words were scribbled in bold, dark ink, the "f" twisted like a salmon breaching out of the water.

I'm coming home for you, Mollie girl.

IN FIELDS OF SNOW FLOWERS

12

IN FIELDS OF SNOW FLOWERS

Willow blew on his numb fingers and glanced up at the dull sky. It had been raining—a steady, weary drizzle—for the past week. A dampness like that gets into a man's bones, no matter how warm it is outside.

Two weeks. Two weeks, and this outfit's commission would be up.

They were a strange crew, cobbled together in the last year out of four companies that were whittled down so small they needed to be stuck together to reach a decent number. There were perhaps thirty or forty men from his original company, no more. The commission jokes flew about the mess and coffee station thick as the mud on the ground, the mud that caked their boots and trouser legs, that dampened the bottom two feet of their canvas tents, that sucked at the hooves of the horses with every step.

When one was urged to join the army, they made it sound like the whole run would be clean-cut. Duty and glory.

This was going out with a whimper. Dying of trench-foot while watching ground nobody wanted. Dying of random bullets because the men on either side were bored, not because they had orders to obey.

"Coffee?"

Willow turned and glanced up. It was a private, holding two steaming tin mugs. "Sure. Thanks."

"Not at all. How's the dawn watch?"

"Holding." Willow smiled briefly. "Not much change these last few weeks."

The private crouched down beside him. "Sure don't see any value in this land."

Willow gave a short laugh and took a sip. "I guess there's just a lot more to it when it's not raining all the time."

"You think we'll make it?"

"We've made it up until now."

"Willow, I mean it."

"I sure hope so."

"What are you going to do? You're not staying?"

"No." Willow pulled his coat tighter about himself. "I was thinking of settling. I don't spend much of my pay—I could probably afford a farm or something eventually."

"A farm?"

"Don't laugh," chided Willow, but he was laughing along good-naturedly.

"I'm going to go home. After six years, maybe my old man has mellowed some. He runs a shop. Tallying goods sounds pretty nice right about now."

"Yeah." Willow drained his cup and handed it back.

"Mr. Tam."

They both turned. One of the captain's orderlies stood behind them.

"Sir?"

"Captain wants to see you."

"Now?"

"Yes. Spriggs here can take your place until you're back."

Willow picked up his rifle and ducked his head under the strap. "See you, Spriggs."

THE CAPTAIN's tent was as neat as a place could be buried under layers of damp and mud and smoke. The captain himself was a man nearing middle age, with the weary look around his eyes that field commanders wore and black hair that was just beginning to turn.

"Sir." Willow saluted with a mud-stained hand.

"Ah, Mr. Tam. Prompt as usual. Your—commission is up in two weeks?"

"Yes sir. One day shy of two weeks."

"Yes, yes." He waved that away. "I understand you marched under Captain Innes."

"I did, sir. In the Northern Frontier."

"I understand you were there all the way up until the end?"

"Yes. I was part of the final expedition north."

"You had commendations written for you. Did you know that?"

That must have been Lieutenant Ransom. He couldn't think of anyone else who would write him one.

"No, sir, I did not."

"Well, it's on your record. Resourcefulness, courage, and clear thinking under fire. Invaluable assistance in specially written reports to the peace efforts between us and the Uniak."

"Yes, sir."

"I need a man for a job, and I am giving you a field promotion."

His heart sank, but aloud he said, "Thank you, sir."

"It's necessity. Corporal Hanks is dead—I don't know if you heard that."

"No, sir."

"Just last night. Sniper. Don't tell the men. Anyway, I need a man to take his place. There is a hill, just to the southwest of our line, unoccupied at present, and it seems from what intelligence we have that the enemy wants it. I want you to lead a small company of men—I will pick them for you—and take that hill. I will give you what fire support I can, and I will give you one piece of light artillery with which to hold your position. Is that clear?"

"Yes, sir. When are we to take it?"

"Tonight, as soon as it is dark. Do you have any more questions?"

"No, sir."

"Dismissed, Corporal Tam. Congratulations."

Willow saluted sharply.

Only in the army do they congratulate you as they send you to die.

SEVENTEEN MEN. That's what the captain found for him. Huddled together in a quiet, uneasy bunch, talking a little, drinking more. When a man is faced with death only days from promised freedom, he turns to rum and whiskey like it's water.

Willow coughed, his breath standing in the thick air in front of him. After that series of fevers a couple years back, he'd never been quite the same in the damp.

They were just waiting on the light artillery piece. The captain had said it would be ready for them before dark, but it was dark now and still the gun had not arrived.

"Corporal Tam, what's the holdup?" asked the lieutenant, striding up.

"We were promised a light gun."

"Oh. About that—the captain's decided he doesn't want the men weighed down. Proceed as ordered, no gun."

Willow forced cheer onto his face as he saluted. "Sir."

Then he turned to the men.

"We're heading out now. Closed ranks, do you hear? Rifles at the ready, do not fire unless fired upon, and silence in the ranks. Let's move."

He took hold of the trench ladder and climbed up. A thick mist was creeping over the pocked mud. At least they had that to their advantage.

Once or twice he glanced over his shoulder to make sure the others were close behind. In the dark, he couldn't see more than two rows back.

Face to the front, Willow.

In the trenches it was bad, but in the flat land between the trenches and the hill, the mud was awful. Within minutes he could feel it splashed above his knees, the damp soaking into his worn boots.

He stepped into a length of standing water over a stretch of grass. There was nothing for it—it was wet feet or a bullet. He pushed on, cringing at the noise his feet and the men behind him made splashing through the water.

At the foot of the hill it was a little better. White flowers grew all along the sides, illuminating their footsteps in the dark, making it easier to pick their way along.

Once, he glanced back. The shadowy movement on the pale hill showed they were still moving along.

He trudged on. The good thing about a steep hill was that once you were on top, your enemies would have to make the same climb under fire.

The top was silent, covered in the flowers. They were alone.

"Standard, you set the extreme right. I want you bent so you face southeast."

"Sir."

One by one, the men filed by. Not until he counted seventeen strung across the crest of the hill did he allow himself to breathe again.

"All right. Teams of three. Two dig, one watches."

The men fell into place immediately. No one wanted to spend a minute longer than they had to in an exposed position.

Strange. Standing on the hill, listening to the night sounds with every ounce of his concentration, brought Uniap'nik straight back to him. It was as if he was there again, and any moment now, Iki would shove a cold nose against his hand.

He had not thought of Uniap'nik, not with such startling clarity, in some time.

He wondered how she was doing, that plucky little girl. She would hardly be a girl now.

The trenches were taking form under the men's spades,

marring the once unsullied ground, cutting a swath through the gentle nature around them, piling dirt into a construction of war and destruction.

But destruction that would save men's lives, he reminded himself.

How he wished to be done with the army. Away from this necessary death and destruction.

"Keep it up, men. Good work." It took very little in this strange foggy night for his voice to carry, and the last thing he wanted was for the enemy on their other side to hear.

The work continued as the fog rolled, ghost-like, between the men. Something caught at Willow's senses. A splashing footstep? A cough? He swiveled around, his ears straining for other sounds.

Orange light spat from below as the hill echoed with the crack of rifles.

"Down, men!"

He threw himself into the trench as a dozen bullets lodged in the raised ground with a sickening thud. It was too similar to the sound of a bullet in a man.

The half-dozen men on watch returned fire.

"Load and return fire!" Willow shouted.

The trench was still shallow; once the spat was over, he'd have the men return to work. At least they had gained a few feet of cover before they were discovered.

He pulled his pistol from its holster and took aim.

The skirmish lasted only a few minutes, but from the sounds at the bottom of the hill when the firing ceased, there were quite a few casualties on the other side.

Willow wiped his nose on the back of his hand, let his breath out in a low whistle. "They won't try that again—not for a while, at least."

"Sir." The young man beside him, one Private Thatcher, gave a shaky grin.

"Pass the word to reload and be ready for a second wave."

Thatcher saluted and started down the line, crouching low.

THE NIGHT WAS WEARING thin when they tried again. Bullets whistled over the top of the trenchworks like wasps. It put Willow in mind of a time he had been working a hay field and one of the men had disturbed a ground nest.

Not too different from bullets, those ground bees when they struck you.

A bullet whined past, close. He didn't hear the second one coming, but it stole the breath from his lungs as it tore through his arm, knocking him back.

"Corporal!" Thatcher was at his side immediately.

He pulled himself up, pain blinding him, hands shaking. "It's nothing, it's just my arm, get back to the line." He dug in his pocket for his handkerchief with his good hand.

"Sir, at least let me tie it." He helped Willow with his coat and then wrapped the handkerchief over the wound, pulling it as tight as he could.

"Thank you." Willow replied through his teeth.

"Sir." Thatcher's reply was measured, but his eyes were worried.

"I am not going anywhere, Private." Willow managed a wry smile.

Thatcher returned to his place and Willow set to reloading.

"They're retreating!" The call came down the line, and

Willow propped himself against the top of the trench to fire a few parting shots.

"Corporal Tam, what are we going to do?"

Willow dragged himself up by one elbow and turned to face the muddied speaker, a grim-faced man of about forty, whose eyes were on the ground beyond the hill as he waited for answer.

"Hold the line. The captain wants to keep this hill, so we'll get relief sooner or later. That's what we're up here for —pass the word."

"Sir."

Spriggs came up the line, ducking low, his kit over his back.

"You're bleeding, Corporal Tam. You've got to get that stopped."

"I see that." Willow gritted his teeth and shifted his position.

"I'll do it, if you let me."

"Go ahead."

Spriggs shrugged off his pack, pulling it around, taking out his spirits ration and some cloths.

"You can use my spirits." Willow indicated to his pack with a shaky hand. "I don't have the stomach for them."

Spriggs accepted this with a nod. No time to waste.

"Let me see it." He undid the handkerchief, half stuck to the wound with dry blood.

"Anyone else hurt?"

"A couple minor things, like this. No casualties, nothing serious."

"Good." Willow leaned his head back against the dirt.

"What's the idea of this?" A man's voice broke the stillness. "It's daylight, they can pick us off! Aren't they going to come for us?"

Willow tried to sit up, look to see who was talking.

"Easy now, it's just talk." Spriggs pushed him back and pressed a wet cloth against the wound. "There, it's going to smart a little."

Willow sucked his breath in through his teeth.

"They said there wouldn't be a fight!" Another voice, in agreement with the first. A low rumble of assent from the other men was beginning, like the thunder over the west hill.

Spriggs glanced over his shoulder grimly and proceeded to soak down a cloth pad.

"Just tie it off tight, you can clean it out in a minute." Willow sat up.

"But Corporal—"

"Do as I say, Spriggs!"

THEY WERE IN A HUDDLED GROUP, shivering in their muddied coats with bloodshot eyes from a night of fighting and straining eyes through fog and gunsmoke. Fifteen of the seventeen, all but the watch.

"I want to make something clear to you men, right now." Willow cleared his throat, sought a moment for the right words.

"What we are told and what happens is not always the same. So it goes with anything in life. So I tell you what we are going to do. They are going to relieve us—it's not a matter of if, but when. In the meantime, we are going to hold this hill. We are going to eat what we have, pass around the coffee, sing if we must, and we are going to make the last days of our commission as brave as any company has before us. Is that clear? We'll make the enemy sorry coming and going."

They gave him a low chorus of agreement.

"So get those fires going. They're not taking anything from us, do you hear? We're men of the Fourteenth Company!"

"Yes, sir!" called one of them. The others started to cheer, chanting "fourteenth."

"Come on, sir." Spriggs appeared at his side again, like magic. "We've got to get to that arm."

THE RAIN HAD STARTED AGAIN, but the fires and the hot coffee held the chill at bay. The men were wrapped in their thick coats, cleaning their guns, watching the line. Nothing had been heard all morning from the enemy line below.

Willow was beginning to doubt that there even was a line below. He hoped it didn't mean they were gathering their forces. Even well entrenched, there wasn't much they would be able to do against a regiment.

Down the line, one man had a lit cigar, and he was passing out a couple more, broken in half, to the few lucky men around him. One man started a snatch of song—he had an unsteady tenor voice but a good ear. A few of others joined in, their voices thin in the thick, damp air.

I was just a farmer's lad
Nothing fine 'bout me.
But they said it'd be my making
If I joined their old army.

I took the coin and swore the oath
And now I'm eating mud!

A smattering of laughter met this substitution and the singer grinned as he went on:

Last man picked and first to die,
That's the way a soldier goes.

So rally to the standard now,
Take your place by me.
We'll run the foe around the point
And die some other day.

WILLOW PICKED up the song with them on the second verse, and the men lit up at their officer—newly appointed as he was—joining them.

"How you holding, sir?" Thatcher settled himself on the fresh dirt.

"Fine. Hardly notice this old thing."

That wasn't exactly true, as the arm was stiff and painful, but Spriggs had done a good job cleaning the wound, and as far as he could tell, it was decently clean.

"I sure am getting sick of this rain."

Willow gave a small laugh. "It makes the flowers grow. Or so my mother used to say while she lived."

"I didn't know she was gone."

"I came back from the Northern Frontier, went on leave, and she was sick. Glad I had those few days with her."

"You got anybody now?"

"No." Willow draped his arm over his knee. "At least,

not around here anymore."

"Well, I still have my brothers. They all went into sensible professions." He laughed half-heartedly at his joke. "Don't know what else I have. I might reenlist."

Spriggs came over, holding out a tin mug. "Corporal, I brought you coffee. How's the arm?"

"Fine."

Spriggs took the liberty of moving his coat to check, and Willow shifted away. "It's no different."

"You're our commanding officer. I have to check," Spriggs replied grimly, replacing the coat and backing up. "If it starts to feel feverish, you tell me."

"What good will that do?" Willow attempted a smile.

"You tell me." Spriggs's voice was stern. "Sir."

MORNING DAWNED with a headache and more rain. No relief had come.

"The orders stand," Willow told the men that morning, still crouched in their heavy coats in the drizzling rain. "They'll come when they can. In the meantime, we show that enemy we're not afraid of them."

The men sang again as the coffee was passed around. The sound—any sound—hurt his head, but he wasn't going to stop them.

Hang it all, he could die of this headache, and as long as the men held in good spirits, it would probably be worth it.

He coughed and it caught at his lungs, deeper than before.

"Sir." Thatcher met him at the extreme right. "There's movement below."

"Ours or theirs?"

"Theirs, I think."

Willow dug his field glasses from the wide pocket of his coat. Sure enough, on the southeastern edge of the field, movement disturbed the white of the flowers.

It didn't make sense, holding this hill. Holding without any support or backup. It was foolhardy, and they were in a bad position.

The only thing he could think of was that somewhere someone had made a mistake, either in sending them or in not having infantry support sent after them.

And here they were, foot soldiering in the mud, at least half of them used to cavalry work. It was bad enough for those men to work dismounted, but to be stuck in a siege position like this—well, relief had better come, because he didn't know how he was going to keep the men's spirits up.

He coughed again, smothering it, then pocketed the glasses as another racking cough seized him, bending him double.

"Sir, are you all right?"

"Just a cough." He took a deep breath and straightened.

They needed relief before he sickened worse.

ALL DAY he had wrestled for the men's spirits, even as they fought and repulsed two attacks from the enemy. Mud and blood caked every man until it was hard to tell one from the next.

Two men were dead. He was feverish. He had informed Spriggs—only Spriggs—and the man had offered him medicine. But it was a dulling sort, the kind that took the pain and your clarity of thought, and he had turned it down.

Maybe this would be his death, within sight of his commission running out, but he'd have discharged his duty to the fullest.

He leaned his feverish head against the cool mud. Hard shivers racked his shoulders. He was trying not to let the men see, but he could hardly keep his head up anymore. His arm throbbed like it was on fire.

At least—at least there was no sight of the enemy below, just fields of snow flowers, stretching as far as one could see, defying the mud.

Snow flowers, like the snow, like the clean, crisp air of Uniap'nik. It was a pity he'd never get a chance to return….

"Private Spriggs."

"Sir?" Spriggs's voice was oddly gentle. Odd…odd, that.

Willow shook himself. He had to stay alert.

"Inform me of any changes. Change the guard on the hour."

"Sir, you should be resting."

A chill wormed up his back and seized his shoulders. "I'm all right."

"You don't look it."

"Look—don't tell the men, but just in case, if I fall asleep and don't wake up, you're in charge, do you hear?"

"Is your arm that bad?"

"It's that and an old fever cropping up. Blasted damp. Are those orders clear?"

"Yes, sir."

"Good."

He drew his coat tighter around his aching shoulders and shifted so he could look down at the fields again.

The sun was going down.

He drank in the fading light. It was a nondescript gray on the horizon, not even a sunset, but it very well could be his last day, and he wanted it while it lasted.

His eyes were heavy.

The men, you have to stay awake for your men. The thought fought off the darkness again and again.

His limbs grew heavy. He could feel himself going limp; each time his body fought to stay awake, to fight against the racking chills, it left him with less strength to struggle.

Perhaps this was how a man drowned, slowly drained of fight until the dark water overtook him.

Shadows moved over the white of the flowers, white like the frigid snows of that northern territory where they froze their bones, but they had each other—saints, they had each other.

Shadows. He pushed himself up on one shaking arm, raised his voice. It was hoarse, his voice—he needed water.

"Spriggs?"

"Sir, what is it?"

He gave a nod to the shadows of men—there must have been forty of them—materializing on the hill.

"Have the men muster. Tell them to repulse the attack. Don't shoot until they can see clearly, understood?"

"Sir."

But Spriggs stayed.

"I said tell the men."

"Sir—" Spriggs nodded to the shadows. "Those are our men."

. . .

"Corporal Tam, it is men of your courage and resourcefulness that keep Irylia free and prosperous and safe from her enemies. If you were to change your mind, I could recommend your field commission be made permanent."

Willow stood at attention in the captain's tent, his arm in a sling, his face worn but his uniform immaculate. His dismissal papers lay on the desk under the flickering light of the lantern.

Two weeks in the army hospital had put him back on his feet, but with warnings to go somewhere with better air for his health. He was now nearly five days past his expired commission.

"Thank you, sir, but I am finished."

"I understand. There will of course be extra compensation, one for your condition, and second for your work on Tanner's Hill. The commanders were impressed."

"Thank you, sir."

The captain stood, straightening the papers and folding them in clean, neat lines.

"Here you are, Corporal Tam."

Willow accepted them silently.

"Is there anything else I can do for you?"

"No, sir."

"In that case, dismissed." He saluted, and with an effort Willow raised his arm from its sling to return it.

He stepped out of the tent into the muggy air where an orderly waited with his horse. Mist was rising from the muddy ground, but the sky had finally cleared and there were stars, silvers stars hung in the dark blue blanket of sky.

He wanted cold, bracing air. He wanted mountains, leagues and leagues of them, and birch trees and wildflowers in spring. He wanted to fish in wild, clear streams and live where a man could hear himself think.

Out there on the hills, with the flowers spread out below him, the idea had started in his mind. Now it was clear as day in his heart.

It was time to go home.

WITH THANKS

When I write a standalone novel like *Seventh City*, I rarely have a desire to explore the world or characters further. Even I, the author, am only privileged to look through a window at these characters during a certain time in their life, and most of my questions I have to let be.

You, the readers, woke this desire and made it possible for me to press further into this world for more answers and more stories. This one's for you.

To Elisabeth, thank you for pouring your heart and expertise into me and my stories. I hope we get to keep telling stories til' we're a hundred years old.

To James Egan, I don't know how you manage to be this awesome, but every time I think you can't top the last cover, you do. Thank you so much.

To Esther, whose art gives me great joy. Thanks for bringing Maki and Willow to life.

To my proofreaders: Anna, John, Ethan, Alice, and Lydia, I can't even begin to say how grateful I am for your interest and help and keen eyes.

To Merry, whom I love, and who asks if she's in the acknowledgements, thank you for all the little presents you bestow on me while I'm writing.

To my street team, you guys are amazing. Thank you for all your enthusiasm. I love getting to share stories and geek out with you.

To my family, thanks for being there and for celebrating the wins with me.

To my Heavenly Father, from whom all blessings flow. Thank you for the rain shower.

An exclusive preview of
THESE WAR-TORN HANDS

Coming June 2021

I

THERE IS rain-smell in the air tonight. The wild air—barely moving enough to stir the territory flag across the street—quivers with it.

I can remember when this land was wild nothingness. No town, no roads, meager and dusty as they are. I was there before there was anything.

I lower myself into the rocking chair on the porch, lean my back against the slats. Somewhere far off, I hear a bellow. Certainly it is someone's bull, but I am in a fanciful mood tonight, and I can almost imagine that it is a *darani*. Those that are left are mostly in the hills now, dwelling in the deep caves, nursing their ancient reptilian grudges, no longer common dangers.

The territory is new. The governor even newer. But this—this town—settlement, more like—is a spark of civilization where once not so long ago was a windswept plain, teeming with unpleasant ways to die.

Humans are fascinating creatures. Clinging to patches of earth where frail things like them have no business being, insisting on seeing beauty in the most desolate and terrible of places. There is a compass in their hearts, and against all sense, they follow the point of the needle.

Usually to their deaths, but sometimes to greater things.

And it is for the greater things that I have been waiting. Waiting like the barren hills for rain.

I fish my pipe from my pocket, raise my boot over my knee to strike a match against its sole.

But the pipe doesn't settle me tonight. Rather, it makes me unsettled.

Governor Scott is young—too young, in the minds of the men in tall hats out east. Against all their arguments for an older, heavier-handed man, he was chosen. But what do they know?

Archer Scott is as much a piece of this land as the sagebrush.

I was there then, too, when he was born. It was I who laid him upon his dying mother's chest to ease her passing. It was I who gave him to a grim trapper with a quiet Auki wife.

She was the only woman in the territory then. Thirty-six years ago, that was. Now there's sixteen, and more coming.

Oftentimes, it is not the doctors, nor the bankers, nor the politicians who flock to a place like this, so remote and disconnected from the rest of the world. Not until there is something of substance to hold them fast to a space of earth so wild that the wind would blow you off, come a fortnight. No, the men who come are those who have nothing to lose, everything to gain.

But when this territory was newly bought—a pin's price to the Auki and Red Tree clans, who lived nearest and wouldn't set foot on it—I was there.

And who says that I ever came? Perhaps I have been here, old as the hills, from the beginning of time, waiting for something. Something I can feel in my bones.

The wind snaps the flag like a woman shaking out a tablecloth.

There is a storm coming.

EMILY HAYSE is a lover of log cabins, strong coffee, and the smell of old books. Her writing is fueled by good characters and a lifelong passion for storytelling. When she is not busy turning words into worlds, she can often be found baking, singing, or caring for one of the many dogs and horses in her life. She lives with her family in Michigan.

www.emilyhayse.com

facebook.com/theherosinger
twitter.com/theherosinger
instagram.com/songsofheroes
goodreads.com/theherosinger

Manufactured by Amazon.ca
Bolton, ON

22005523R00134